Kissing Maggie Silver

By Sheila Claydon

Amazon Print 978-1-77362-747-2

Books We Love
A quality publisher of genre fiction.
Airdrie Alberta

Copyright 2013 by Sheila Claydon
Cover Art by Michelle Lee
All rights reserved. Without limiting the rights under copyright reserved above, no part of this publication my be reproduced, stored in or introduced into a retrieval system, or transmitted, in any form, or by any means (electronic, mechanical, photocopying, recording, or otherwise) without the prior written permission of both the copyright owner and the above publisher of this book.

Dedication

For Ellen
This one's for you

Acknowledgements

Thanks must go to Lesley Fleming for reading the manuscript of *Kissing Maggie Silver* several times and making her usual invaluable comments, Michelle Lee for designing the perfect cover, Roxanne Nolan for her scrupulous editing and helpful suggestions, and Jude Pittman and Jamie Hill at Books We Love for their continuing advice and support. Without them, my writing life would be considerably more challenging.

Chapter One

The noise blasted Ruairi's ears the moment he pushed open the swing doors. He recoiled instinctively. Too many people! Too much music! Even too much food! He looked at the laden tables and his stomach protested. After six months working in what had to be one of the most peaceful places on the planet he was finding it more difficult than usual to readjust to the demands of civilization. All he wanted to do was to back out of the room and leave.

Leaving wasn't an option, however. So, ignoring his momentary discomfort, he turned to the small, gray-haired woman who was standing beside him.

* * *

"Can you see anyone you know?" he asked.

"Over there!" She pointed, and then set off at speed across the room, adding her own voice to the hubbub.

He gave a smile of satisfaction as he watched her greet and hug her friends. It was time his mother started to enjoy herself again. She had been alone for too many months since his father died.

* * *

"Ruairi O'Connor! I don't believe it! I thought you were in the middle of Africa or somewhere. Don't tell me my parents invited *you* as well as the rest of the world?"

Ruairi grinned at the man standing stocky and square in front of him. "Not exactly. But they invited Mum and she isn't up to travelling by herself."

"So you've crashed the party?"

"I guess!" Ruairi stuck out his hand and then changed his mind and pulled the shorter man into a bear hug. "It's been too long Mark."

"Tell me about it!" Mark Silver hugged him back. Then he broke away and frowned. "Look, it's fantastic to see you again but I can't stop to talk now. I'm under orders to keep things running smoothly. You'll stick around though won't you, so we can catch up?"

Without waiting for an answer he nodded towards a large group of people on the opposite side of the room. "Good! Now grab a drink and then come over and say hello to the rest of the family."

Dodging small children and chattering guests, Ruairi followed him, and within moments he was being welcomed with open arms into the bosom of the Silver family.

"I can't believe it's been ten years since you visited us," Cathy Silver, Mark's mother, still pretty despite her sixty-plus years, shook her head in mock reproof as she smiled up at him.

He gave her a contrite grin. "Sorry Cathy, but you know me...ever the rolling stone."

"Yes, well at least you're here now. We were so pleased when you phoned to tell us you were bringing your mother over from Ireland. She would never have come on her own."

"I know," his smile faded as he acknowledged the truth of her words. Since his father's death eight months earlier his mother had spent far too much time alone in the cottage they had moved to when he retired; a cottage that was more than a mile away from its nearest neighbor and, because she couldn't drive, a long and inconvenient bus ride to the local market town.

After the funeral she'd accepted he had to return to his job in New Zealand and told him she would be fine. And every time he'd telephoned she had sounded fine. That was why he had been so shocked by her appearance when he finally made it back to Southern Ireland. Somehow, despite all she had been through, he'd expected her to be the same. He hadn't anticipated her extra wrinkles and the dark circles under her eyes. Too wrapped up in his career it had been much easier to believe what she told him when he called rather than spend time thinking about how she was actually coping.

When he saw how she had aged and how everything seemed to be an effort, he was consumed with guilt. And it was that guilt that had prompted him to book two return airfares to

England the minute he'd seen the ruby wedding anniversary invitation pinned to her kitchen notice board. He hoped the grief that had overwhelmed her would loosen its hold a little if she spent time with old friends. Isolated for too long, she had lost her natural joy de vivre and become a shadow of the mother he had known all his life, and he was determined to do something about it.

He hadn't discussed it with her. He'd just pulled a couple of suitcases down from the loft, dumped them onto her bed, and told her to pack. When she'd remonstrated he had been blunt.

"You can't let Cathy and John down Mum. They go way back, and besides they took the trouble to fly over for the funeral and then stay on for a few days after Dad died."

Not subtle, or even kind, but it had been effective. She had packed without complaint after that, even allowing him to lock up the cottage and deposit the keys with her nearest neighbor without a word of protest. She hadn't spoken much on the journey to the airport, nor while they waited to board, but once they were on the plane some of her animation returned, and by the time they booked into their hotel she was closer to her old self.

Although he was delighted, it had made him feel doubly bad about his neglect. If a change of scene was all it took, then he had better do something about it. Upgrading their rooms to a suite he told her they were having a holiday. She'd shaken her head doubtfully.

"You can't do that. What about your work? You must have a thousand things to do. Bringing me over for a long weekend is enough Ruairi. You have your own life to lead."

If only! Pushing away the thought that had recently started worming itself into his consciousness at the most inopportune moments, he assured her he had all the time in the world. Later, after she had retired for the night and left him sitting alone in front of the flat screen TV in their suite, he'd been forced to confront the fact that although, to all outward appearances, he had one of the most exciting jobs in the world, he didn't actually have much of a personal life. Nor did he have anyone to share it with.

A decade of moving from country to country as he pursued his career as a wild life photographer had given him a rootless existence that left little time for friends let alone an intimate relationship. There had been girls of course; more girls than he wanted to remember, but none of them had been special. They had just been someone to spend a week with, or a few months with, before he moved on to another country and another contract.

Now, absorbed into the noisy, affectionate warmth of the close-knit Silver family, he wondered if it was time for him to rethink his life and contemplate doing something else, something that didn't keep him away from any possibility of a normal family life for months on end.

A melee of small children playing some sort of noisy game in the middle of the room interrupted his thoughts. If they were all part of the Silver family then it had grown a great deal in the past ten years. He turned back to Cathy.

"All yours?" he asked, pointing.

"Most of them. Peter has four, Mark and Andrew both have two, and there's another one on the way."

"And Maggie?" Ruairi had warm memories of the youngest member of the Silver family. When he last saw her she'd been a skinny, redhead with pigtails and freckles. Considerably younger than her three brothers she had spent most of her time trailing after them, desperate to be included in their games.

"Ah Maggie!" A shadow flitted across Cathy Silver's face. Then the smile was back. "Right at this moment I think she's concentrating on being the world's best aunt!"

She gestured towards the laughing children. Ruairi followed her pointing finger as an older girl emerged from the huddle of bodies and made a break for the garden. Barely glancing at her he searched for someone with a passing resemblance to the young Maggie he had last seen ten years earlier. Then it dawned on him. The slim figure who had just disappeared *was* Maggie. She was the girl with the cloud of pre-Raphaelite curls, curves in all the right places, and an extraordinary turn of speed.

"That's Maggie!"

"Yep! She's brushed up quite well considering, hasn't she?" Mark was back at his side, his duties over for the time being. "She's always in her element at parties like this. She uses them as an excuse to ignore the fact that she's a grown up. I guess that's why the children all love her to bits."

* * *

"...and they all lived happily ever after." Maggie finished the story with a flourish and then sat back and folded her arms. "Now vamoose the lot of you! Go on! It's time to get some food."

Her nieces and nephews grinned at her, even the tiny ones. That was what they liked about Aunt Maggie. She didn't try to be nice or anything soppy like that. She said it as it was, and right now she was telling them she'd had enough. They rushed off to grab paper plates and napkins without a backward glance.

"Well that's thanks for you!" Her sister-in-law, hot and uncomfortable from the late stages of pregnancy, sank onto the bench beside her with a sigh of relief.

Maggie laughed. "I'm used to it. Teaching has shown me that the words gratitude and children should never be used in the same sentence!"

"I don't know how you do it," June shook her head. "You work with them all day long and yet you're still up for playing with them whenever there's a family gathering. You're a marvel Maggie Silver and I wish I had half your energy."

"Well it's easy for me isn't it? I get to give them back to their parents and go home for some peace and quiet. Looking after them 24/7 is a different proposition altogether."

"I guess," June smiled at her and then grimaced. "Ouch! This one kicks every time I sit down."

"Not long now," Maggie said soothingly. "Is there anything I can get you? A glass of juice or something to eat?"

"No thanks. I've got to pay yet another visit to the restroom in a minute, something else I'm looking forward to waving goodbye to along with the heartburn and backache. I just came over to check that you really don't mind taking care of the children when I go into labor. It's a big ask and I'm sorry if Mark sort of forced you into it by discussing it in front of your parents."

"Don't be silly. Of course I don't mind. And when has Mark ever forced me to do anything? Besides, I'll enjoy having the children to myself for a day or two."

"Oh Maggie, thank you! You've taken such weight off my mind. I couldn't believe it when I found out your parents were going to be away for most of August."

Maggie laughed. "Poor Dad! He booked the cruise ages ago as a surprise for Mum for their fortieth wedding anniversary. When he told her about it this morning and she said she had already agreed to look after Amy and Sophie when you have the baby, he really thought he was going to have to cancel it. You know what she's like. It's always family first. He was really upset but trying hard not to show it when Mark popped in to talk about today's arrangements and heard all about it. I'm really glad he talked to me and we managed to sort things out before she refused to go."

"I know. That's why I'm so grateful. I would have hated if they had cancelled."

"Well worry no more, just be glad this baby is arriving during the summer vacation when I'm free. I'll keep my cell phone switched on all the time so you can call the instant you need me."

She frowned as she watched her sister-in-law walk away. June was Australian and her parents, who lived in a remote area north of Brisbane, rarely saw her. Maggie was sure it must be awful to be so far from home and family at a time like this.

Thinking about distant places brought her squarely to the one thought she had been avoiding all afternoon. Ruairi O'Connor. She had seen him the moment he entered the room, as had every other female, young and old, she shouldn't wonder. It had been difficult not to, of course, because he was half a head taller than anyone else. And when he had smiled at her brother Mark she was sure the combination of square white teeth, clear hazel eyes and tan skin had provoked a universal sigh.

Ruairi O'Connor was at her parent's party and nobody had told her he was coming. Ruairi O'Connor who had been the love of her life from when she was seven years old until he went travelling, and broke her heart, when she was thirteen. Ruairi O'Connor who she hadn't seen for ten years because he hadn't ever managed to make it back to any of her brothers' weddings. Ruairi O'Connor who, after a few postcards, had forgotten about her altogether.

Already halfway through a game of hide n' seek she'd had to abandon any thought of speaking to him as she hightailed it through the French windows into the large garden while her eldest niece counted to ten. And now here she was, still in the garden, trying to pluck up the courage to go and say hello to him and hope he wouldn't remember how lovesick she'd been.

It would be so embarrassing if he remembered the countless times she had loitered around his garden gate waiting for him to arrive home from school; or how she had fought to sit next to him whenever he came to hang out with her brothers. And she certainly hoped he wouldn't remember her cuddling up to him if a television program they were watching was too scary, determined to stick it out if it meant she could be with him. But he'd never complained. Not once. Instead, he'd shown her abandoned birds' nests and empty eggshells the color of the spring sky, and helped her to identify the wild flowers in the field at the back of their gardens; a field that was full of modern houses now but which, all those years ago, had been a children's paradise of long grass, insects and tiny scuffling creatures.

Maggie had only been allowed to go to the field if her brothers would take her, and more than once Ruairi had overridden their objections and held her hand all the way there and back.

And he had always been interested in her drawings too. He'd even pretended to be grateful whenever she'd given him a lopsided sketch or a smudged painting, and had propped them against a stack of books in the tiny room his family used as a study; the room where he kept his collection of animal photos, each one meticulously labeled on the back. No wonder she had given her childish heart to him.

She gave a wry smile as she closed her eyes and lifted her face to the warmth of the late afternoon sun. That had been then, when the entire world had been exciting and nothing was impossible. Things were different now. For a start she had grown up and learned that life goes on even when dreams get trampled on, and that hearts broken in childhood mend.

* * *

"You look as if you need a drink!"

His voice was deeper than she remembered but it still had the same edge, as if he was going to smile at any moment. Her eyes snapped open.

"Hello Maggie."

She looked up at him, shading her eyes. He was a dark silhouette against the bright sunshine that was filtering through the trees. He was holding a glass of chilled white wine in one hand and a dish of strawberries in the other.

She hoped she sounded cool and sophisticated as she answered him. She knew she looked very different from the child who had fought to hide her tears as he set off on his travels. Then she had been a skinny teenager with braces on her teeth and freckles on her nose. Now she turned heads when she walked into a room.

He bent down and placed the wine and strawberries on the bench beside her. "I've been waiting for a slot in your busy schedule. Those nephews and nieces of yours have been keeping you occupied for most of the afternoon."

She shrugged, aiming for casual nonchalance. "The result of teaching primary I guess. It's sort of expected of me at family gatherings like this."

He lowered himself onto the grass at her feet, and now that she could see him clearly she noticed he was frowning. "It hasn't given you much of a chance to talk to the other guests."

"Not really my thing at the moment."

"Oh?"

She hesitated and then shrugged. Even after all this time he was still someone who had once seemed to be a part of the family, so what did it matter if she told him how things were in the Silver clan at the moment.

"I've upset everyone because I've just broken up with my boyfriend. He was suitable husband material you see. Apparently Mum and Dad were hoping we'd get engaged in time to turn today into a joint celebration, so keeping out of the way is a good idea."

Ruairi raised his eyebrows, the hint of laughter back in his voice. "I hardly dare ask, but what is suitable husband material?"

"Oh, you know! Kind, considerate, solvent, good with children, the usual stuff."

"So whatever was it that made you turn such a paragon down?"

Maggie shot him a startled look. "You know you're the first person to ask me that. Everyone else just keeps telling me why I shouldn't have done it. Especially Mark because he introduced us."

Ruairi didn't comment. He just waited for her answer.

She frowned. "I don't know why I'm telling you this but if you really want to know it was because he was boring...no, that's not fair. *He* wasn't boring but what he wanted was boring. I'm not ready to settle for a life five miles away from where I was born before I've had a chance to see a bit of the world, maybe work abroad for a while. Mum and Dad were too nervous to let me go backpacking when I was a student, so I want to travel now, before I settle for suburbia. The trouble is, nobody else in the family thinks it's a good idea. They all consider it's time I grew up and settled down. They think I'm being frivolous and irresponsible."

"But you're going to pack your bags and leave anyway?" Ruairi said.

"Like you did, you mean?"

He heard the sarcasm in her voice and smiled at her. "Oh Maggie! Don't tell me you haven't forgiven me yet. I was twenty-one and eager to take on the world. I couldn't hang around for a twelve year old, even if she did have a crush on me."

There it was. Out in the open. Not a hidden embarrassment any longer. Their eyes met and his were full of laughter, and then Maggie was laughing too as the years peeled away and Ruairi was just Ruairi, instead of a tall stranger with heart stopping looks.

"Thirteen! I was thirteen!" she said indignantly.

"So you were," he chuckled.

"And I didn't have a crush…well only a little one," she conceded as his smile grew wider.

* * *

They shared the strawberries and Maggie forgot she was aiming for cool sophistication as they began to reminisce. Tears of laughter washed away her makeup and gave her a severe bout of hiccups when Ruairi reminded her of a particularly amusing incident from the past, and by the time a shout from Mark told them to come and listen to the speeches it was as if the intervening ten years had never been.

"It sounds as if we have to join the party." Ruairi stood in one fluid movement, picked up Maggie's glass of wine, and held out his free hand. She took it automatically and let him pull her to her feet. As her fingers curled into his he grinned down at her.

"You haven't grown much have you?"

Letting go of his hand she bent down and scrabbled under the bench she'd been sitting on until she found the shoes she had kicked off when she started playing with her nephews and nieces.

"I can do tall," she told him indignantly as she slipped her feet into them. Then she spoilt it by getting one of the four-inch spiky heels stuck in the soft turf of the lawn.

Ruairi roared with laughter as he slipped his arm around her waist and half carried her across the grass. He was still chuckling when he lowered her onto the stone terrace and then bent and rubbed the soil from her shoes.

"Thank you," she said with as much dignity as she could muster.

"You're welcome Maggie Silver. Now let me escort you inside." He straightened up and, with a teasing smile, offered her his arm.

Maggie took it with an answering grin but as they made their way inside she was surprised to find herself suddenly feeling as bereft as she had ten years earlier. Worse in fact, because back then she had been sure, with the optimism

19

of the very young, that he would come back for her. Now she knew such thoughts were mere fantasy and that Ruairi O'Connor would probably disappear from her life forever once the party was over.

Chapter Two

Forty minutes later, toasts and speeches over, Maggie looked around for Ruairi. She saw him across the room talking to her brothers.

With the easy familiarity of the past he had kept her arm linked to his while they listened to the speeches. Not until she was needed for the obligatory family photo that would mark the occasion for posterity did they break away from one another. When they did Maggie was surprised at the reluctance she felt as she walked away from him. Even now her fingers carried the memory of the muscular strength of his arm beneath his light summer jacket, while her brain was imprinted with the warmth of his smile and those laughing hazel eyes.

She scowled. She was just being melodramatic. Sure he was attractive, any woman with a pulse could see that, but it didn't mean she had to relive her childish crush. She was twenty-three year's old for goodness sake, and she had plans for the future that didn't include getting heartsick over a man, any man, for a very long time. If she was going to travel and work abroad then she needed to be flexible and fancy free.

Trust Ruairi O'Connor to disappear for ten years and then reappear just when he wasn't wanted. If he was invading her thoughts like this after a couple of hours in his company, then the sooner he went away again the better as far as she was concerned.

"Maggie, over here!" Mark was beckoning to her.

She pasted a smile on her face and made her way across the room. "Isn't it great that Ruairi's here," she said brightly when she reached him. "You must have so much to talk about."

"Yeah, well that's why I need to ask another favor."

"You want me to take June and the children home so you can have a drink with him," she could hear it coming.

He looked startled. "How did you know?"

"I just guessed."

"Well you guessed right. Mum and Dad have decided to end the evening quietly with a few friends. It's been a long day for them, for all of us, and it's past the children's bedtime. Pete and Andy are taking their families home on their way to Ruairi's hotel but I don't want to leave June alone after a day like this, especially as I might be late back."

Maggie glanced across to where her sister-in-law was sitting. She looked wan and tired and far from able to cope with the two small children tumbling about in front of her.

"Of course I'll stay with her. She looks all in. Just give me time to say hello to Mrs. O'Connor and then we can go."

"Thanks sis, you're an angel."

"An irresponsible angel for refusing to get engaged to Graham, apparently." She couldn't resist the dig.

Mark looked uncomfortable. "Maybe I shouldn't have given you such a hard time. It's just that he's a friend of mine and he fits in with the family so well. He had such a lot of plans for both of you too. We thought you were good together, thought you were both set for life, so it was a real shock to all of us when you turned him down. "

Maggie wasn't quite ready to let him off the hook. "I know it was and I'm sorry I upset him, but it's his own fault because he never bothered to check out his plans with me. I kept telling him I wasn't ready for a mortgage. I said I wanted to see the world for a bit before we settled down. I even tried to persuade him to do the same but he wouldn't take me seriously. He just laughed and echoed what Mum and Dad and the rest of you keep telling me. He said I needed to grow up."

"He did?" her brother was definitely squirming now.

"Yes! So I told him if that was really what he thought of me then he'd better find someone more mature to domesticate."

"You didn't exactly finish on good terms then?"

Maggie sighed. "Not really. You know me and my temper, but I'm sorry because I did like him *and* he was your friend."

"Hey don't worry about that. I guess I just didn't realize how serious you are about travelling. Maybe you should ask Ruairi to help you plan a trip. There can't be many places in the world he hasn't visited."

"Ask me what?" Ruairi broke away from the conversation he was having with her other two brothers and came to join them.

"I was just saying you're probably the best person to help Maggie to organize a travel plan, seeing as how you've been everywhere and seen everything."

Ruairi pulled a face. "I wish! It doesn't matter which country I visit I still spend most of my time staring down a camera lens in the middle of nowhere."

"That's a no then?" Maggie teased as she turned away. She was going to ignore the memory of her ridiculous childhood crush and pretend that the last thing in the world she wanted to do was grab his arm again, just to feel him close to her.

"I didn't say that," he protested. "We can talk about it later."

"Whatever," she gave a casual wave as she looked around for his mother. She found her talking to an elderly couple who had once been her neighbors, but as soon as she saw Maggie approaching she made her excuses and opened her arms wide.

Maggie rushed straight into them knowing that Marie O'Connor was the one person in the world who wouldn't criticize her for refusing to settle down. The older woman hugged her tightly for a long moment and then held her at arm's length and smiled at her.

"I always said you'd turn into a real beauty and you have. Look at you! Although how you manage to have that wonderful Celtic coloring when the rest of your family has brown hair is a mystery to me."

"You always said it was because the fairies put a spell of enchantment on me when I was a baby," laughed Maggie. She still cherished the memories of the times Ruairi's mother had invited her into her cozy kitchen and fed her rock cakes, warm from the oven, or Irish soda bread dripping with honey

"So I did," Marie O'Connor's warm Irish lilt had become more pronounced since she'd moved back to the country of her birth. "And maybe I was right because someone certainly bestowed the gift of beauty on you child."

Maggie flushed with pleasure and then hugged her again. "How are you? It seems ages since I last saw you, and I'm so sorry I didn't make it to Mr. O'Connor's funeral but I was in the middle of my final exams so I couldn't get away."

"Bless you my dear, I didn't expect you to come all the way to Ireland. The lovely condolence card you sent me was enough."

She paused and thought for a moment and then she smiled. "And I'm fine. I didn't think I was but I am, thanks to Ruairi. He bullied me into coming over for the party and it's made me realize I've got to stop feeling sorry for myself and start to think about the future. In fact I might even move back here. Rural Ireland was a dream for Tom and me, but now I'm alone and so far from all my old friends, maybe it's not such a good idea."

"I know Mum would love it if you lived nearby again," Maggie said. "In fact we all would. It's not the same now you don't live next door."

"Well perhaps I'll talk to Ruairi about it while we're here. He's insisted we stay on for a bit of a holiday although I'm not sure he can really spare the time. But you know Ruairi, always determined to have his own way. He was never any different even when he was a baby."

"Every time I catch up with you Maggie Silver, the person you are with is talking about me!"

Too engrossed in their conversation, neither of them had noticed Ruairi approaching. Now he stood in front of them, a wry smile on his face.

"Would you look at him," his mother's smile was full of pride. "Such a waste to keep that face hidden behind a camera when he's better looking than most film stars."

Maggie grinned at Ruairi's obvious embarrassment but before she could answer,

Mrs. O'Connor continued. "You too my dear. You don't want to hide your looks away either. I must say you'd make a lovely couple. Together you'd turn heads wherever you went."

"Now there's a thought," Ruairi murmured. "Perhaps we can talk about it when we discuss your travel plans later on this evening."

He had fully recovered from his own discomfiture and was enjoying the fact that Maggie's face had turned scarlet.

Cursing her blushes Maggie shook her head as she gave a brisk response. "Sorry, no can do. I'm taking June home and helping her put the children to bed so that you men can get together for a drink. Mark doesn't want to leave her alone after such a busy day."

A frown creased his forehead. "I'm sorry about that Maggie. When Mark suggested we all meet up for a drink I thought you were coming too. It won't be the same without you. Is there no one else who can stay with your sister-in-law?"

"'Fraid not! Her family lives in Australia, and anyway Saturday is not the best time to find a last minute babysitter. Besides you really don't need to worry about tail end Maggie tagging along anymore Ruairi, because now she's all grown up and can look after herself. "

"If you say so." Although he was smiling, the jut of his jaw made his irritation obvious. For a moment Maggie wondered if she had been a bit too flippant about his invitation, but as he turned to speak to his mother she dismissed the idea as ridiculous because he had never been someone to take offence over a triviality. Maybe he wasn't just being polite. Maybe he really did want her to join him for a drink.

As she watched him Ruairi slipped his arm around his mother's shoulders. "Cathy and Ian have invited you back to their house for the evening Mum. I've ordered a taxi to collect you at eleven but if you want to stay later just ask Ian to telephone the taxi firm. He has the number."

"Thank you dear." Mrs. O'Connor turned and beamed at Maggie. "You see! I told you he bosses me about but I'll do as he says because I'm having such a lovely time. You will come and have lunch with me before I go back to Ireland though won't you? There are still so many questions I want to ask you. I want to know how you like teaching because the last time I saw you, when Tom and I came over for a visit, you were still at college."

"Of course I will," Maggie gave her another hug. "I'll call you tomorrow but right now I must go and rescue my sister-in-law. Her baby is due in a few days so the party has been a bit much for her. She looks absolutely worn out."

"I'll come with you to say goodbye," Ruairi fell into step beside her and soon he was helping her to transport sleepy children, bags and balloons into a waiting taxi while June searched out Mark and his parents to tell them they were leaving.

Once the children were safely strapped in he turned and looked down at Maggie. "I really am sorry you won't be there this evening you know."

She shrugged. "I don't expect it crossed Mark's mind that you were inviting me as well. You know I was only ever included under sufferance."

"Maybe. But that was then. I'm much more interested in the here and now and whether you will have dinner with me on Monday evening?"

She shook her head, ignoring the sudden rapid beating of her heart as he took a step closer. "You don't have to do that Ruairi. You don't have to be kind to me or look after me anymore."

"I rarely do anything I don't want to do," the irritation was back in his voice. "For goodness sake Maggie, I'm not asking you because your brothers forgot to invite you tonight; I'm asking you because I want to have dinner with you."

June and Mark's appearance interrupted whatever answer Maggie was about to make and it wasn't until both women were settled into the taxi that Ruairi got a chance to speak to her again. He ducked his head through the passenger window just as the driver started the engine. In the fading light his eyes looked bottle green. His voice was low, aimed solely at Maggie.

"I'll call you tomorrow…about dinner," he said.

* * *

For the next hour Maggie was too busy to think about Ruairi. She bathed the children and read them a bedtime story. Then, the bathroom tidied, she collected their discarded clothes and took the pile downstairs to the washing machine. Once it was loaded she went into the sitting room to check that June was still sitting comfortably in front of the television with her feet up. She smiled when she saw that her sister-in-law had fallen asleep and quietly retreated to the kitchen to prepare a light supper for them both.

Despite her best efforts, slicing tomatoes and grating cheese didn't take her full attention, and she soon found her thoughts drifting back to Ruairi. Did he really want to take her out to dinner or, despite his protests, was he just being kind because Mark hadn't included her this evening? She wished she knew.

She wished she knew, too, exactly how she felt about him. Her initial embarrassment about her childish crush had quickly evaporated as he teased her about the past, and she had soon found herself responding to him as she had always done, merely replacing childhood chatter with a more sophisticated repartee. She couldn't believe how quickly she had told him about her non-engagement and her travel plans either. It was as if she had been saving up words until he reappeared so she could share them with him.

That had been what had made him so special when she was a child, she remembered. He had always been ready to listen, had always been able to make sense of things for her and to find ways to boost her confidence when her brothers put her down.

And that's what he's doing now, she told herself. He knows I'm everybody's least favorite person at the moment, so when he saw how Mark didn't even think of including me this evening, he decided to take me out to dinner instead to make me feel better about myself. Well I won't go! He's not going to be around for more than a couple of weeks anyway, so why give myself unnecessary heartache? If I see him when I have lunch with Mrs. O'Connor then all well and good, but I'm not going to let him treat me like a child who needs looking after.

She broke the eggs for the omelet with unnecessary force and then crashed saucepans and cutlery in a fury of angry frustration. When she returned to the sitting room with June's supper on a tray, her sister-in-law was wide-awake. She grinned at her.

"Did you win the battle?"

Maggie gave a shame faced smile. "Sorry! I woke you up didn't I, with all that clashing about?"

"Yes, but it doesn't matter. I only needed twenty minutes to recharge my batteries. What's more important is whether you've decided to have dinner with Ruairi O'Connor or not."

Maggie gave her a startled look. "Is it that obvious?"

"Only to me. Everyone else was too busy enjoying the party to notice anything, but because my unwieldy bump more or less kept me in one place I spent a lot of time people watching, and I saw you and Ruairi. I was also in the car when he said he'd call you, in case you didn't notice!"

"I didn't think you heard," Maggie said.

"I'm not deaf Maggie, just pregnant. Come on! Tell me what it's all about. It's obvious you like one another, so why all the angst?"

"Oh…it's all so complicated." Maggie pushed aside her half eaten omelet and flopped back in her chair. "When we were children I thought Ruairi was wonderful, more than wonderful in fact. I had a full-blown crush on him that lasted for years. I guess everybody knew and probably found it funny, but at the time I thought it was my secret. And he was always so kind to me. He never seemed to get fed up with me hanging around, and when Mark and the others teased me he often stuck up for me and insisted they let me tag along too."

"So he's a nice guy…so where's the problem?"

"That's just it," Maggie groaned. "He's still a nice guy and he's still expecting them to let me tag along, so when he realized I wasn't going to be with them this evening he invited me out to dinner instead."

"Are you sure he said instead?" June asked her. "Because from where I was sitting he seemed to be really enjoying your company."

"Well no, he didn't actually say instead, but it's obvious isn't it?"

"Not to me it isn't. How long is it since you last saw him?"

"Almost ten years. And for the first few months after he left I really did think he'd broken my heart. You know what teenagers are like, all developing bodies and rioting hormones. I think I quite fancied myself as the abandoned lover actually."

June laughed. "You mean I've got that to look forward to with my two girls?" Then she shook her head. "Have you actually looked at yourself in the mirror lately Maggie? I mean, come on! When Ruairi left you were nothing but a kid, so of course he treated you like one. But from the way he was looking at you this afternoon I think he's got the message that little Maggie is all grown up and quite the woman these days."

Maggie shook her head. "From the way he was teasing me I know nothing has changed. He still sees me as little Maggie, someone to take care of for a week or two until he sets off on his travels again, and I'm not prepared to let him do that. I'm not going to let him break my heart all over again."

* * *

Much later, in bed and unable to sleep, Maggie remembered June's words and sighed. What if her sister-in-law was right and Ruairi really did find her attractive. Where did that get her? Into a short relationship that's what, and then he would be off across the world and she would never see him again. No! Her first instinct was right. She was definitely not going out to dinner with him, not unless everyone else came too.

Chapter Three

Her cell phone rang early the following morning while she was searching under her bed for a lost shoe. She wriggled backwards on her stomach but not far enough so that she banged her head when she tried to sit up. She was still cursing and rubbing the bruise when she picked up her phone.

"It doesn't sound like a good morning at your end," Ruairi chuckled. "Did you get out of the wrong side of the bed?"

"No, I was crawling out from under it," she said ruefully, wishing her heart hadn't done a sudden back flip at the sound of his voice. She was feeling irritated with herself because, in the clear light of morning, she knew she wasn't really going to refuse his dinner invitation at all despite of her protestations to June. At some time during the night her heart had overruled her brain and now the only thing she wanted to do was to see him again.

"How's your mother?" she asked, playing for time.

"She's fine although she is a bit tired today. She really enjoyed yesterday though. Meeting up with so many old friends did her good."

"I'm glad. I'll phone her this afternoon to arrange a lunch date for later in the week."

"Well that's partly why I'm calling. Yesterday she was buoyed up by wine and excitement; today she's feeling a bit sorry for herself. She's worried that you don't really have time for lunch. She thinks you were just being polite when you agreed to meet her. I told her not to be so silly but she says she's too old for someone as young as you to want to bother with her, so I'm…um…sort of moving things along."

Maggie sank onto her bed, horrified. "Surely she knows I'm looking forward to spending some time with her. She was like a second Mum to me when I was small. Why on earth would she think I'm just being polite Ruairi?"

"Probably because she's spent too much time alone since Dad died. She's forgotten that there are people who love her. She hasn't made many friends in Ireland because Dad became ill almost as soon as they got there so all her time was taken up with nursing him."

"In that case she definitely needs to move back here and I shall tell her so when I see her this lunchtime," said Maggie firmly, completely forgetting her angst about Ruairi as her warm heart went out to the woman who had been so kind to her when she was a little girl.

She heard the smile in his voice as he replied. "Shall I tell her one o'clock?"

"No! Tell her twelve. Then we can have a drink first. Maybe that will prove to her that I really do want to see her."

"Thanks Maggie. And on Monday evening it's dinner at six. I'm afraid your brothers have pre-empted my invitation by organizing an early meal for everyone at the local Chinese restaurant. Apparently it's a send off for your parents on the night before their cruise, which is why it's so early. Marks says they have a plane to catch later in the evening."

"Fine," said Maggie, too brightly. "I'll be there."

* * *

That'll teach you to be careful what you wish for she told herself crossly as she ended the call. Now you can go to dinner with Ruairi O'Connor without any worries at all. With your dear devoted brothers around there is no chance he'll ever see you as anyone but their aggravating little sister, so situation solved.

She wished he hadn't proved her point so thoroughly though. She had spent hours fretting about how her heart would cope on a date alone with him and now he had made it pretty clear that he had been quite happy to include everyone else all along.

* * *

Despite her irritation about Monday's plans, she thoroughly enjoyed her lunch with Marie O'Connor. The older woman was interested in everything that Maggie had done since she last saw her, and she wanted to know about her plans for the future too. As Maggie had known she would, she understood completely why she wanted to travel before she settled down, although she could also see the other side of the story.

"Your family are upset because they don't want to lose you," she said when Maggie told her how everyone was reacting to her plans. "They'll worry about you all the time you're travelling, whereas if you'd agreed to get married to Graham you would have stayed close by and been safe."

"But that's ridiculous!" Maggie's stormy grey eyes flashed with irritation. "Staying put has no guarantees at all."

"I know that only too well my dear," Marie O'Connor shook her head sadly. "But believe me I also know how your family feels. When Ruairi first decided to travel it broke my heart."

You and me both, thought Maggie with an inward sigh.

"I behaved like a fool. I was so sure he would have a terrible accident and I'd never see him again that I could hardly eat for weeks before he went. Then, once he'd actually gone, I spent every spare moment waiting for a postcard or a phone call, and I can tell you they were few and far between because he was a young man with the whole world to see. Of course when he finally came home for a visit and I realized he was a man, not the young boy I still held in my heart, I stopped worrying so much. Finally I understood I had to let him go."

"And now?" Maggie suddenly wanted to talk about Ruairi, wanted to learn everything there was to know about him.

"Ah, now." She looked wistful for a moment before she continued. "Now he's seen everything he ever wanted to see, he has a career he loves, he's successful, and yet despite all that, I know he's not happy. Sometimes I see such a sad look on his face that it breaks my heart."

"But why?" Maggie asked, surprised at this sudden insight into a man who appeared to be so confident and cheerful.

"Oh he's not going to confide in me my dear. He might tell you though." Suddenly she grabbed Maggie's hand. "That's it! He always talked to you didn't he? Maybe you can find out what's wrong and help him."

* * *

"Just great!" muttered Maggie twenty minutes later as she left the hotel. "Now I'm being set up as Ruairi's counselor! Well it's so not going to happen when I can't even counsel myself."

She was so busy thinking about her dilemma as she retrieved her sunglasses from her bag and pushed them onto her nose, that she failed to notice someone approaching from the opposite direction until she bounced off a very hard chest. A strong arm stopped her from falling but her glasses were knocked askew and she dropped her bag.

"Ouch! That hurt!" She glared up at her assailant.

Ruairi grinned down at her. "Maggie Silver, always in a hurry to get somewhere. Nothing has changed then."

She didn't deign to answer. Instead she bent down and started retrieving all the things that had spilled from her bag. Ruairi joined her, grabbing pens and makeup from under the feet of the people walking by.

"I hoped I'd catch you," he said as they stood up. "I've a favor to ask."

"Ask away." Maggie was very glad the bright summer sunshine gave her an excuse to keep her sunglasses on. That way she could feast her eyes on him without giving anything away about what his proximity was doing to her pulse rate.

"If you're not doing anything else this afternoon would you look at some apartments with me?"

For a moment her heart leapt. Was he going to stay around after all? He soon dashed her hopes.

"Johanna, a girl I worked with in New Zealand, is flying in next week. I promised I'd find somewhere for her to stay but as I spend most of my life in a motor home or a tent when I'm filming, and in a soulless hotel when I'm not, I'm hardly the best person to ask. You'll have a far better idea of what another woman would like than I would, so if you have a couple of hours to spare I'd really appreciate another opinion."

There had to be a girl!

"What is she looking for?"

"Oh you know, the usual thing. Not too expensive and with good transport links to the city. Ideally she wants a couple of bedrooms, a kitchen and living room plus access to a garden, although at such short notice she knows she might not get everything she wants. I've lined up a few possibilities with a local estate agent."

With no plans for the rest of the day and unable to think up a plausible excuse in the time it took Ruairi to open the door of his hire car, Maggie had mixed feelings as she settled herself into the passenger seat. She wasn't at all sure her blood pressure was going to be able to cope with spending a couple of hours in such close proximity. She twisted her head slightly so she could watch him from behind her sunglasses.

He was studying a local map; checking out the travel routes for this girl that Maggie already hated; so she was able to watch him at leisure and linger over every detail. His hair was a long, long way from red she decided, and yet it wasn't quite brown. It was the warm rich colour of a horse chestnut. And he was big, much bigger than any of her brothers. Big, and tanned, and...

41

His eyes, a clear hazel and fringed with long, gold tipped lashes, were full of laughter as he turned to speak to her. "Well, do I measure up?"

She flushed, angry with herself that she had let him see her staring. What was the matter with her that instead of acting normally, like she had when they first met yesterday, she was letting the memories of her silly schoolgirl crush take over?

"Sorry, I was miles away," she lied. Then, ignoring Ruairi's chuckle, she turned away and watched the traffic out of the window. The rest of the journey passed in silence and by the time he drew up outside a shabby redbrick building she had regained her composure.

"This doesn't look very promising," she said, as they negotiated broken paving stones in the garden path.

Set back off the road, the property was surrounded by a crumbling wall, while all that remained of the gate was a forlorn and rusty hinge. An estate agent was waiting for them, key in hand. She introduced herself and then led the way inside. The interior was just as awful as Maggie had predicted and they were outside on the pavement again within five minutes.

The next three apartments were all equally dispiriting and it wasn't until they pulled up outside the last address on the list that things began to improve. Climbing out of the car Ruairi looked approvingly at a large detached house set in a neat garden.

"This looks better," he muttered in Maggie's ear as they waited for the agent to unlock the door.

A tour had her green with envy for the unknown Johanna. The house had recently been divided into four separate apartments, one of which was still vacant. It had the latest kitchen and bathroom fittings, polished wooden floors and pale walls. Maggie loved it all. If she had been looking for an apartment of her own then this was exactly what she would have chosen, right down to the view of the enclosed garden through a wide picture window.

"I love it," she said, forgetting for a moment that she despised domesticity and intended to travel.

By the time she left them it was quite clear the agent thought they were moving in together. "I'm sure you'll be very happy here," she said, shaking hands with both of them. "I'll be in touch as soon as the tenancy agreement is ready for signature."

"She thinks it's for us," said Maggie crossly. "You could have put her right about that."

Ruairi grinned at her. "Maybe I didn't want to. Maybe I wanted her to think I was moving in with a beautiful girl even if she does have a black scowl on her face. It's good for a man's ego you know…besides I'm not that bad a prospect. I am housetrained!"

Maggie decided to ignore the picture his words conjured up in her mind. She didn't want to think about sharing anything with Ruairi. She didn't want to think about Ruairi full stop. It was time to change the subject.

"What's she like anyway?" she asked. "Johanna, I mean. What's she like?"

"Jo? Tall, fair hair and blue eyes just about covers it. Oh and she's a zoologist. That's how I met her. She was working in a conservancy area where I was filming."

Great, thought Maggie gloomily as she climbed into the car. Now it's Jo and she's not only tall and blonde, she even works with wildlife, just like him. Well if she ever meets me she'll realize she's got absolutely nothing to worry about because an undersized primary school teacher is no competition at all.

Ruairi, unaware of her despondency, was studying the map again. "I knew it. Look, there's a park at the end of this road," he said, pointing. "Let's find somewhere to sit for a while you tell me all about this travel plan of yours."

* * *

They didn't discuss her travel plan though because when they reached the park they were greeted by shrieks of delight as three of Maggie's nephews flung themselves at her.

Their father, Maggie's eldest brother Peter, greeted them with surprise. "Whatever are you two doing here?

"I asked Maggie to help me with a spot of house hunting for a friend," explained Ruairi. "I needed a female perspective."

Peter's answering laugh was edged with pointed sarcasm. "You also needed someone with an interest in making a home, someone looking to put down roots. And I'm afraid my dear sister fails on both those counts."

For the briefest of moments Ruairi's eyes met Maggie's. Then his gaze flicked back to Peter, and although she knew it was just something to do with the light, to Maggie they appeared to lose their green and gold flecks and become a dull, muddy pond color.

"Maggie was very helpful," he said, putting a slight emphasis on the word very. "And nobody can be more rootless than me, not even your sister."

Then he turned his back on Peter and smiled at the children. "Now I'd like an ice cream. Does anyone here know where I can buy one?"

The excited children immediately surrounded him, eager to direct him to the ice cream van parked near the entrance to the park. Peter frowned at the unexpected put down but then he shrugged as Ruairi pulled out his wallet and bought ice creams for everyone.

* * *

Much later, after several ball games, and when the boys had been taken home for their tea, Ruairi lay back on the grass and watched Maggie. She was sitting cross-legged and searching for four-leafed clovers.

"Don't you mind the sniping?" he asked.

She didn't bother to pretend not to understand. "Of course I mind. But there's not much I can do about it is there? If I lose my temper then it's just Maggie having a tantrum. If I stay calm then it's Maggie not caring. I can't win either way. It's another reason why I want to travel. I need to prove to everyone that I'm capable of making a life for myself. I want them all to recognize I'm an adult who doesn't need their continual advice. I want them to realize I'm not little Maggie anymore."

"They must be blind not to see that," he said lazily, resting his head back on his hands. "It was the first thing I noticed at the party even though you were trying to disguise yourself as a ten year old!"

"That's not funny!" she snapped. "Don't make a joke of it Ruairi because I am just about fed up with everyone so it wouldn't take much to add you to the list."

He sat up and put his hand on her arm. "Slow down! I wasn't joking Maggie. Don't you know how beautiful, clever and full of spirit you are? It shines out of your face, all of it…so why do you let them do it? Why do you let your brothers take advantage of you? Why do you let them treat you as a sort of joke?"

"I guess because they always did," she said unsteadily, hoping he would take his hand away before the imprint burnt straight through her skin and on, down towards her heart.

He heard the tremor in her voice, saw the glint of tears on the end of her eyelashes, and felt an unexpected surge of anger. How could they treat Maggie like this? Dear sweet Maggie who had been like a little sister to him all those years ago. Without thinking he slipped his arm around her shoulders and pulled her to him, just as he would have done when she was a child. At the same time he put his free hand under her chin and tilted her face upwards. He had been going to say something soothing to her, words that would persuade her out of her sadness. It wasn't until their eyes met that he realized his mistake. He had told her he had seen from the first that she wasn't little Maggie anymore but it hadn't been true, not until she was in his arms. Now, with her face inches from his own and her wide grey eyes glittering in the sunlight, he discovered she was very grown up indeed and there was only one thing he wanted to do. He wanted to kiss her.

Chapter Four

Maggie went back to her search for four-leafed clovers. Anything was better than looking at Ruairi. For the briefest of moments, no longer than it took to draw breath, she had been so sure they were going to kiss one another that without thinking of the consequences, she had moved a little closer, her lips parting in involuntary anticipation. Instead, he had just given her a brotherly hug before taking his arm away and leaving her squirming with embarrassment.

Out of the corner of her eye she could see him stretched out on the grass, apparently asleep. So much for his insistence that, in his eyes at least, she had grown up. If he really believed it then surely he must have seen the naked longing in her eyes, for somehow, in the pause between one heartbeat and the next, Maggie had started loving him all over again. And she knew that this time it wasn't just the whimsical imaginings of a lonely child.

Ruairi watched her through the curve of his eyelashes. He couldn't believe it had taken him so long to recognize that Maggie had indeed stepped across the threshold of childhood. There was nothing of the leggy teenager left at all. He gazed hungrily at her heavy curtain of copper hair, aching to thrust his fingers into it and pull her to him, to feel the slender lines of her body up close and personal, to crush the rosy pout of her full lips under his. If only!

The old Ruairi O'Connor would have had no compunction in following up such a sudden and unexpected desire with action. But this was Maggie. She wasn't someone who could just share a part of his journey. Any involvement with Maggie would be forever, and there was no way he was close to being ready for forever with anyone.

He knew Maggie couldn't be a few weeks in a foreign city, or a month or two on location. She was already too much a part of him. Despite barely thinking of her for years he was surprised to discover how deeply the memories of the young Maggie were twined around his heart. Maybe, without realizing it, he had just been waiting for her to grow up. Maybe bringing his mother over from Ireland to the one party where he was sure to meet Maggie again was some sort of subconscious act.

Maybe rubbish! He was deluding himself. Just because the nomadic existence that was part and parcel of the career he had chosen had gone sour, he was looking for a solution. And right at this moment he wanted Maggie to be that solution because she was lovely, and funny, and warm, and achingly familiar as well. If he was finally going to admit to himself that after years of crisscrossing the globe he was lonely, then he wanted Maggie to be the balm that would heal his emotional void.

Meeting up with the Silvers and being absorbed into the warmth of their extended family had opened up a well of loneliness deep inside him that he hadn't known existed. He gave an inward sigh as he slanted another glance at Maggie's bent head. He was being ridiculous. It was just proximity that was making him think this way about her. He would feel differently tomorrow. He always did. In a few weeks his feet would get itchy and he would be impatient to move on. In the meantime though, he needed some down time, and surely Maggie was the ideal person to spend it with. He just needed to stick with friendship and not look for anything else because, apart from the fact that he wasn't ready to get tied down, Maggie herself had already made it abundantly clear that she wasn't looking for any sort of relationship with anyone at all. She had just escaped a brush with suburbia, something she appeared to consider a fate worse than death, and she intended to stay footloose and fancy free while she travelled the world, and who could blame her? Not him, that was for sure. She wasn't much older than he had been when he'd settled for a rootless life lived through a camera lens. And if he was totally honest, until recently he hadn't regretted it at all.

* * *

Maggie was late for the O'Connor/Silver reunion dinner the following day. It wasn't exactly deliberate, more a case of taking too long to decide what to wear, but beneath her dithering was a streak of childish defiance; a deep down annoyance that, as usual, nobody had thought to check whether the evening's plans fitted in with her own. Even Ruairi had just assumed she would be happy to meet up with him before her family had hijacked their dinner date.

Serves you right for not telling him no when he first asked you, a little voice in her head admonished, but Maggie didn't feel like heeding it. She preferred to hug the unfairness of it all to her chest, anything to counteract the feeling of embarrassment that flushed her cheeks every time she thought of Ruairi and that moment in the park.

Irritated with everyone and everything, she kept her spine straight and her head high as she stalked into the Chinese restaurant. It was a wasted effort though because nobody was watching. They were all too busy chatting and laughing as they caught up on old times. She slipped into the one vacant chair with a scowl. It was between her two oldest nieces. Aged eight and nine, they had obviously been considered old enough to join the family party and they had saved a place for her between them. Her scowl deepened. Much as she loved them both she wasn't in the mood to entertain them. The only thing going for it was that it meant she was sitting as far away from Ruairi as possible.

With a sigh she dutifully bent an ear to their excited chatter and despite her irritation, by the time the meal arrived the old Maggie had won through. It always did when she was with children. She forgot her temper as she helped them to choose portions of food, and then they all got the giggles as they tried to use chopsticks.

"Maybe we should give in and use the spoons," she suggested, watching her nieces chase grains of rice around their bowls.

"That's the coward's way out," Ruairi's voice cut across the chatter of the table, forcing her to look up and acknowledge what she had known all along, that although she wasn't sitting anywhere near him, their chairs were on exactly opposite sides of the large circular table in the one place where they were in direct eye contact. Determined that he shouldn't know about her earlier embarrassment, she lifted her chin at his challenge. He grinned at her and raised a morsel of food to his mouth with perfectly balanced chopsticks. Then her brothers joined in, and soon the whole table was full of exclamations and laughter as everyone ate their food Chinese style with varying degrees of competence.

Maggie's display of over-the-top enthusiasm as she encouraged her nieces and brushed up her own skills, was for Ruairi's benefit. She wanted him to think she was busy and happy with her plans for the future, plans that didn't include him or anyone else sitting around the table. It was the only way she could contain the heartbreak that was building inside her all over again as she listened to him telling stories about his travels. With each word she remembered anew how she had felt all those years ago when he had first told her he was going away.

Her ploy worked though. Watching her slowly become the life and soul of the party on her side of the table, Ruairi silently acknowledged that Maggie didn't appear to have a care in the world, anymore than he had had when he first went travelling. He had been right to ignore the sudden surge of attraction he'd felt when they were in the park because it was the wrong time and the wrong place for both of them. Soon they would be on opposite sides of the world again, as far apart as it was possible to be. As he forced himself to bring his attention back to the table, he wondered why the thought was so unexpectedly painful.

* * *

By the time the evening ended everyone was tired and the two little girls were almost asleep as they snuggled up against Maggie. She smiled down at them as her brother Andrew came around the table to collect them. "Come on sleepy heads, time to go home."

They went with barely a protest. Nor did Andrew's muttered thanks raise a response from

Maggie. Suddenly she didn't care anymore. Let her family treat her as an unpaid babysitter; let Ruairi think what he liked. Soon none of it would matter because she was going to find a job a long way away; somewhere where teachers were desperately needed; somewhere that would be such a challenge she wouldn't have time to think about anything else. Not that she had started looking yet, but she would. She would start tomorrow.

She pushed her chair back as everyone else started to search for bags and jackets. She was going to leave now before Ruairi had a chance to speak to her. Out of the corner of her eye she could see him walking across the room towards her and she had no intention of letting him break down her defenses again. She was going to forget how he had rekindled her childhood crush and concentrate on her plans for a new life. Hurriedly she made her way to where her parents were standing and gave them both a hug.

"Enjoy the cruise," she said. "And don't worry about June and the children. I'll look after them, and Mark will let you know the minute the baby arrives."

"Maybe it will be late," her Mother said hopefully.

Mrs. O'Connor heard the wistful remark and laughed. "Not a chance of that from the look of her. This is one time you're going to have to let your family manage all by themselves, Cathy, my dear. Now off you go and forget about everything. Ruairi and I will be around for most of the time you're away, so we can always lend a helping hand if necessary."

* * *

While everyone else congregated on the pavement so they could wave her parents off in the taxi that had arrived to take them to the airport, Maggie slipped back inside the restaurant and asked the receptionist to order her a taxi to take her home. Then she visited the cloakroom; anything to keep her as far away from Ruairi as possible.

She had just finished washing her hands when Mrs. O'Connor appeared. "Oh there you are Maggie. Ruairi sent me to find you because our taxi has just arrived."

Maggie forced a smile as she gave her a hug. "It's been a great evening hasn't it? Thank you so much for helping us give Mum and Dad such a wonderful send off. Tell Ruairi goodbye will you, and I'll call you in a day or so to arrange another lunch unless you'd rather do something else. Maybe you'd like to go shopping or something."

Mrs. O'Connor returned her hug with a laugh. "No! No! You don't understand my dear. The taxi is for the three of us. As we are all travelling in more or less the same direction it seemed a waste to pay for two taxis, so Ruairi cancelled yours."

Maggie was so taken aback that she didn't immediately reply and by the time she found her voice Mrs. O'Connor was already disappearing through the door. Without any other choice, Maggie followed her, fury building inside her at the sheer effrontery of Ruairi's behavior. It certainly hadn't taken him long to start to treat her just the same as everyone else.

When they reached the pavement, he was waiting, holding open the door of the taxi. She let him help his mother in before she turned on him.

"I can't believe you've just cancelled my taxi," she said, keeping her voice as level as she could. "How dare you assume I'm just going home. You could at least have taken the trouble to ask me about my plans…I could be going anywhere. I might even have a date."

"But you're not and you haven't," his voice was infuriatingly calm. "You told the receptionist where you were going Maggie. I wouldn't have done it otherwise."

He made it sound so reasonable and, to her chagrin, Maggie did now remember giving her address to the girl behind the desk. She also knew the taxi would pass her front door on its way to the hotel. She wasn't about to let him off the hook though.

"But how do you know I haven't changed my mind?" she challenged, suspecting she sounded like a brat but beyond caring.

"Have you?" Ruairi asked. "Because if you have then you can take this taxi and I'll order another one for Mum and me. On the other hand, if you haven't, then I hope I can persuade you to come back to the hotel with us for a grown up drink. I absolutely promise there won't be anyone under the age of twenty-three in sight."

"You noticed," Maggie muttered, her temper ebbing away against her will as she realized that, far from taking her for granted, he was trying to make up for the fact she'd spent the entire evening at the kindergarten end of the table.

"I noticed. Now are you coming with us, or do I need to order another taxi because I think the driver of this one is getting just a little bit impatient?"

"Coming," she said. And she slid into the seat beside Mrs. O'Connor without another word.

* * *

The sitting room of Ruairi's hotel suite was huge and luxurious. With a twinge of envy she sank into one of the comfortable chairs and accepted his offer of a glass of wine. Mrs. O'Connor gave her a conspiratorial smile.

"If you don't mind my dear, I'm going to say goodnight and go to bed. I'm not used to all this socializing and although I hate to admit it, it's beginning to wear me out."

She put up a restraining hand as Maggie started to get to her feet again. "No, don't get up. You stay there and have a lovely long chat with Ruairi. There must be so much you want to talk about after all these years, so much catching up to do. And get him to give you some travelling tips too, Maggie. That way you can persuade your parents that you know what you're doing when you set off on your adventure. It'll stop them worrying quite so much while you're away."

So this is when I'm meant to ask Ruairi what is bothering him I suppose, Maggie watched the older woman close the door with a twinge of irritation. Really, Mrs. O'Connor was too obvious for words.

Besides, as far as she could tell, Ruairi was absolutely fine; in fact he was better than fine. So far she hadn't seen any sign of the sadness his mother had mentioned. If anything his mood was annoyingly calm and upbeat. She was willing to bet *he* had never had a tantrum in his entire life.

* * *

Unsettled, she got up and walked across to the window to look at the view. Although the sun had set, there was still just enough light to see the boats on the river and the outline of the trees on the riverbank.

"What a lovely view," she said, and then realized she sounded more like a passing acquaintance trying to make conversation, than a friend. Recognizing that if she didn't shape up she would look ridiculous, she squared her shoulders and turned towards him.

He was watching her. When their eyes met he raised his glass. "Here's to your travels. Are you going to tell me about your plans now or over a meal later in the week?"

"We've just been out for a meal," she said, knowing she still sounded ungracious.

If Ruairi noticed, he didn't comment. Instead he shook his head. "If you mean the dinner date your family hijacked, then that doesn't count. Nor does the time we spent at the park, because Peter and his children were there too!"

Against her will, she laughed. "Don't assume you'll have any better luck if we do go out for a meal. My family is all pervasive."

He leaned forward and topped up her glass. "In that case we need to stay one step ahead of them. Let's make it lunch tomorrow instead of dinner. Then we can drive out into the country and find somewhere a bit off the beaten track."

Reluctantly, Maggie shook her head. "I can't do that because I'm on call for when June goes into labor. I've promised her I won't go anywhere too far away."

"Well in that case…." Maggie's cell phone interrupted Ruairi's reply.

It was her brother Mark.

Chapter Five

Mark opened the front door and sprinted down the path while Ruairi was still paying the taxi driver.

"Don't let him go," he called. "Ask him if he can take us to the hospital. We need to leave straight away...the baby, June...it's all happening a bit too quickly!"

Hearing the panic in his voice, Maggie ran past him, into the house. June was kneeling at the bottom of the stairs, panting hard. She looked up when Maggie arrived though, and smiled at her.

"I'm fine. Don't forget I've done all this before. And Mark will be fine too once we get to the hospital. He just doesn't fancy acting midwife!"

Maggie laughed, relieved her sister-in-law was in control of the situation, and impressed too. She couldn't imagine being so calm if it was her baby that was coming.

"Tell me what to do," she said. "Do you need anything? Are there any last minute instructions?"

"No. I've every faith in you Maggie. I...." June paused as another contraction gripped her. Then Mark was there, helping her up and keeping a protective arm around her shoulders as they walked slowly down the path.

"Don't forget this," Maggie ran after them with the suitcase they had left in the hall.

Ruairi took it from her and lifted it into the trunk of the taxi. "I've already paid the fare," he told Mark. "It'll save you time when you reach the hospital."

"Thanks...thanks...I'll catch up with you later," Mark was concentrating on June too much to really take in what Ruairi was saying.

Maggie wasn't though and she gave him her first genuine smile of the evening. He was still the old Ruairi. The one who looked out for all his friends, not just for the irritating little girl who had insisted on dogging his every move whether he liked it or not. The thought loosened the knot in her heart. If he could be this generous then so could she. She would ignore the fact that her silly childhood crush was trying to take over her life again and just be his friend. That way she could enjoy his company while he was here and worry about the fall out later.

Ruairi returned her smile and then they stood together and watched the taxi pull away. He turned to her as it disappeared around a bend in the road.

"I guess we're going to have to scrub our lunch date, then!"

Maggie grinned up at him. "I told you nothing in my life is sacrosanct to my family, although even I didn't think they would sink so low as to use childbirth as an excuse."

Ruairi was still chuckling when they reached the front door. "How about we give up fighting it and meet up again tomorrow anyway, all four of us? I imagine pizza will go down well with the children."

"You'd really do that? You'd really take Sophie and Amy to lunch as well?"

"Of course. Besides it seems that including at least some of your family is obligatory if I want to see you."

"In that case, we accept…and pizza would be lovely. I just hope you don't live to regret it," Maggie's face was alight with mischief as she wished him goodnight and went indoors to check on her two small nieces.

* * *

As Ruairi walked back to the hotel he tried in vain to banish Maggie's dimples from his mind. They wouldn't go away though, and nor would the memory of her large grey eyes laughing up at him from beneath the tangle of her long copper-colored hair.

By the time he reached his hotel room he was convinced he had taken leave of his senses. Why else had he persisted in asking Maggie out when he knew there was no future in any sort of relationship with her? For a start it had been a mistake to invite her back to the hotel for a drink. One look at her silhouetted against the window had proved that to him, so why hadn't he used Mark's phone call as the ideal opportunity to walk away. Instead, and against his better judgment, he had landed himself with two small children as well, although at least they would act as a wedge between Maggie and his own questionable intentions. Having them around would ensure he could face himself in the mirror in the morning in the same way it would ensure the time he spent with Maggie remained strictly platonic. He also knew it was going to take every ounce of his will power to keep it that way, so he didn't have the first idea why he was putting himself through it.

By the time he climbed into bed he still didn't have an answer.

* * *

Maggie's day started at six o'clock the following morning when Amy, her three-year-old niece, found her parent's bed empty and started to cry. Maggie, hearing her sobs, climbed out of her own bed and went to look for her. She found her weeping on the landing, a pink cotton rabbit clutched to her chest.

"It's all right sweetheart. Mummy will be back soon. She's gone to the hospital because your new baby is ready to come out of her tummy now." Maggie smoothed back the little girl's fluffy curls as she rocked her to and fro.

The noise woke up Sophie who was five-and-a-half going on thirty. "Stop crying Amy," she ordered. "Mummy told us Auntie Maggie would come if she had to go to the hospital in the middle of the night."

Amy stopped crying and communed silently with the pink rabbit that was her defense against everything scary or strange in her three-year-old world. Maggie waited with baited breath. Sophie sighed with elder sisterly disdain. Eventually Amy turned her head and looked at Maggie with a hopeful expression.

"Rabbit says you're going to read a story," she said.

"Rabbit is quite right," laughed Maggie as she led them back to her own bed, and for the next hour the three of them snuggled close as she worked her way through a lot of stories about princesses as well as a book of nursery rhymes and a tale about a very small owl.

It wasn't until she started clearing away their breakfast dishes that she began to worry. Surely the baby would have arrived by now, so why hadn't Mark phoned? She hoped nothing was wrong.

The sound of his key in the lock brought her to her senses. Of course everything was fine. He probably just wanted to tell the children about the baby himself so, instead of phoning, had waited until June was settled and then come back home. One look at his face as he entered the kitchen told her she was wrong.

"Whatever is the matter?" His appearance frightened her. His face was the color of putty with the dark circles of his eyes standing out in stark relief.

"It's June...and the baby," he fell into a kitchen chair as if his legs wouldn't hold him up any more. "She had to have an emergency caesarean. It all happened so fast. At first things were fine, but as soon as her water broke the doctor started yelling for the emergency team. It was horrible."

"But why? She's never had any problems before has she?"

"No, none at all but this was different. She had...it was...a prolapsed cord or something. The doctor said it doesn't...he said it's quite rare...but when it does happen the baby can die if they don't get it out quickly. Apparently the baby's head can press so hard against the cord during the birth that it can cut off its own lifeline, so they can't afford to waste even a minute."

"They did get it out in time though?" Maggie's question was tentative. She was scared of the answer.

He buried his head in his hands and she heard his voice break. "Yes...he's alive, but there might be some brain damage. We won't know for a few days. He's in the neonatal unit because he needs to have a lot of tests...I... he wasn't breathing when he was born Maggie."

Not sure what else she could do, she walked around the table and put her arms around him. "What about June?" she whispered.

"She's okay," he said, holding onto her. "Shocked of course, and sore, but she's okay. She's just feeling desperate about the baby."

* * *

Much later, after Mark had had a shower and changed his clothes, and Maggie had cooked him bacon and egg and then thrown most of it, uneaten, into the trash can, and Mark had kissed Sophie and Amy goodbye and returned to the hospital, Ruairi arrived.

Maggie opened the door, took one look at his smiling face, and burst into tears.

"Whatever's happened?" his smile changed to alarm when she couldn't answer him. He gripped her shoulders and lowered his head so that his eyes were on a level with hers. "Maggie, tell me what's the matter. Is it the children?"

"No, no they're both fine," she made an effort and pulled herself together. "It's June and the baby."

* * *

Telling Ruairi about June and the birth trauma she and Mark had just been through should have been straightforward, and it would have been despite her stupid tears, except that he kept touching her. First he put an arm around her shoulders and led her inside. Then he kept it there while he pulled out a chair and sat her down at the kitchen table. And as if that was not enough, when he sat in the chair opposite he took hold of both her hands. He was still holding them when she finished her story.

She made no attempt to withdraw them though because the warm feeling that was growing inside her had little to do with the fact that the touch of his fingers was making her heart beat too fast, and everything to do with the fact that he was worried about her. Of course he was desperately sad for Mark and June, but right at this minute it was her he was thinking about, and Maggie, who wasn't used to anyone recognizing she had feelings of her own, was letting it go to her head.

Maggie and her opinions always came way down the list as far as her family was concerned. As far as she could tell they only remembered she existed when she was needed as a baby sitter or it was time to attend a big family party, and they only worried about her when she wouldn't do what they wanted, so Ruairi's reaction to her distress had the opposite effect to what he intended. It made her cry harder, something that left her feeling not only stupid but also very ashamed. How could she even think like this when such a terrible thing had happened to Mark and June? She should be concentrating on Sophie and Amy, not sitting at the kitchen table holding hands with Ruairi O'Connor.

"The girls!" she gasped, suddenly coming to her senses. She pulled her hands free and pushed back her chair. "How could I have forgotten them? I must go and see what they're up to."

Ruairi stood up too and nodded towards the window. "They're playing in the garden. Digging by the look of it."

She swung round. Sure enough, he'd had a clear view of the children the whole time she had been such a sniveling wreck, and he was right, they were digging, quite happily, in their sandpit.

"You see, nothing to worry about. Shall we go out and check with them that pizza is still their preferred dining experience, or would you rather stay here in case Mark comes back?"

"I think it would be better if we took them out," Maggie said after a moment's thought. "They know something's wrong, but not what it is, and until Mark is ready to tell them I think the best thing we can do is distract them." She paused then and gave him a shamefaced smile. "I can't believe I've just spent the past ten minutes ignoring them when I should have been putting them first."

Ruairi rested his arm lightly across her shoulders again as they left the kitchen and made their way out into the garden. "I don't think they noticed," he told her. "And just occasionally you are allowed to put your own feelings first Maggie Silver, or has no-one ever told you that?"

Chapter Six

Considering how the day had started, Maggie, Ruairi and the children managed to thoroughly enjoy themselves.

After pizza and ice cream Ruairi drove them all to the park where he had almost kissed Maggie, and they let Sophie and Amy paddle and splash at the edge of the quiet river that looped and meandered its way beneath the trees. Then, when they had worn themselves out, Maggie and the girls sat under the shading branches of a sycamore tree while Ruairi fetched cold drinks for everyone.

When he returned Maggie was checking her cell phone. She had been checking it regularly all day for texts, or just in case she had missed a call, but there was still nothing.

Seeing the tension in her face, Ruairi was glad his hands were too full for him to do what he wanted to, which was to hold her close and kiss away the lines of strain around her mouth and the frown between her eyes. He gave an inward sigh, pushed straws into the juice cartons for the children, handed one to Maggie, and then drank from his own before making a suggestion.

"Do you think…would it be a good idea if we stopped off at the hospital on the way home so you can go and see June for yourself and find out how things are?"

She hesitated and then nodded. "I'd like that. Anything will be better than not knowing what's going on."

"Come on then," he got to his feet again, picked up Sophie and hoisted her onto his shoulders, tucked a very sleepy Amy against his chest, and set off towards the car park. Maggie, following along behind carrying discarded sandals and cardigans, was more grateful than she had expected to be that she didn't have to do everything on her own. Not that it would be for long because as soon as she could telephone the rest of the family to tell them how things were, they would all rally round. She couldn't do that until June and Mark wanted her to though, and this morning Mark had been very specific when he told her he and June needed time to come to terms with what had happened. He'd said they didn't feel ready to celebrate with lots of visitors, not until the baby had had all his tests and they knew the full situation, so right at this moment it was just down to her and Ruairi.

* * *

Ruairi stayed in the car with the children while Maggie walked through the hospital following the signs to the Neo Natal unit. When she found it, the first person she saw was Mark. He was standing talking to a nurse on the other side of the security door. She tapped on the small observation window and when he saw her he asked the nurse to let her in. He greeted her with a tired smile and a question in his voice.

"Maggie?"

"I just had to know about the baby, and about June too," she told him, searching his face for any sign that things had improved.

He looked shamefaced. "I'm sorry...I should have telephoned, given you an update, asked how you are coping with the girls...it's just that it's been...I mean it's a lot to take in and I don't seem to be able to think of anything else."

"I know," she gave his hand a squeeze. "And Sophie and Amy are fine. They're sitting in the car with Ruairi trying to find out if he has any songs on his iPod that they actually like."

He gave a proper smile then and it washed away some of the strain in his eyes. "Poor Ruairi! After this he'll be glad to disappear into the jungle again, or to where ever his next outlandish outpost is."

Maggie gave a nod of agreement as she resolutely pushed away the thought that when that day came her heart would break, and when it did it would shatter into a lot more pieces than it had when she was thirteen.

"June and the baby?" her gentle question brought him back to the reason for her visit.

"June's with him now. Come and see, although you won't be allowed into the room. I can't go in either dressed like this. I have to put sterilized scrubs on before I'm allowed near either of them."

Maggie followed him along a corridor until he stopped outside some double doors and another observation window. He peered through it and waved when June saw him. She got up from the chair she had been sitting in, next to an incubator, and walked over to the other side of the glass. When she saw Maggie the lines of exhaustion on her pretty face lifted and she smiled and gave a thumbs up sign.

"Does that mean the baby is going to be alright?" Maggie asked as she blew her sister-in-law a kiss.

"Maybe…at least the doctors think so. He has to have quite a few more tests over the next few months but the pediatrician doesn't think there is any lasting damage. Of course he'll have to stay here for a few more days yet." He paused then, as he belatedly realized what that would mean for Maggie.

She shook her head impatiently. "It's fine Mark. I don't care how long I have to stay with the girls if it means the baby is going to be all right."

With a farewell wave to June, they turned and walked back to the unit's main reception area. Maggie reached up and kissed her brother's cheek as a nurse tapped in the security code that would open the door for her. "Don't worry about a thing. Just let me know if you need anything because Ruairi has offered to do the fetching and carrying. And let me know when I can visit properly and hold my new nephew."

He nodded and then turned away, his mind already back with his wife and newborn son, so that when Maggie asked him what they were going to call the baby he didn't hear her through the closing gap of the heavy door.

* * *

Climbing back into the car beside Ruairi she smiled at him. "The pediatrician thinks everything is going to be fine although they won't know for sure for a few months yet."

His smile was as relieved as her own. He turned to the little girls who were scrambling back into the child seats that Maggie had transferred from Mark's family saloon into Ruairi's hire car.

"Did you hear that girls? Your little brother is strong and healthy."

"Just like me," Sophie said.

"And me!" Amy wasn't going to be outdone in healthiness. "And rabbit too," she added.

"You are all very strong and healthy, especially rabbit," agreed Maggie as Ruairi turned on the ignition and backed out of the parking space.

"Does strong and healthy call for a celebration," he asked as they left the hospital car park and filtered out onto the main road. "Because if it does, then I know just the place."

"But we've already been out for lunch," Maggie said. "Besides it's nearly the girl's bedtime."

Then she realized where he was taking them and began to protest in earnest. "No Ruairi, not to your hotel. We all look like ragamuffins. We're covered in grass stains and ice cream, and Sophie and Amy aren't even wearing their shoes. You can't possibly take us there."

"Watch me!" he chuckled as he turned the car sharply into the entrance of the underground car park and found an empty space near the hotel elevator.

"Now everybody out because this hotel makes special food for hungry little girls, and besides, I know there's someone here who will want to hear all about your new baby. And about your day in the park too," he added.

Maggie gave in. "You really are a glutton for punishment," she told him and then laughed as Sophie and Amy scrambled up into his arms as if it was the most natural thing in the world, leaving her to collect all the debris of their day and trail behind them again.

* * *

When the elevator stopped at the ground floor to collect more passengers, the first person they saw as the doors opened was Marie O'Connor.

"Gracious me, am I about to have company?" she asked, as she joined them in the lift, her face wreathed in smiles.

"We're going to have tea," Amy told her, hanging onto the collar of Ruairi's polo shirt as she swiveled round to talk to her.

"Well that's really lucky because I'm so worn out from shopping that I need a cup of tea myself, so maybe we can look at the menu together and you can help me to choose a cake to eat with it."

As she spoke to the children her eyes were full of questions and as soon as they left the lift Maggie told her about June and the baby while Ruairi walked ahead of them with the children clinging like limpets to his shoulders.

"Poor June," she murmured. "I know how she feels because I've been there, except my baby didn't recover. Tom and I had a little girl when Ruairi was four. She was beautiful. We called her Colleen, and when she was born we were so happy. Then the doctor told us there was something wrong with her…that she had a heart defect…he said she would only live for a few weeks."

She turned and looked at Maggie, her eyes full of tears. "He was wrong though. She survived for almost a year. She was such a happy baby too, and so good. It was almost as if she knew she wasn't going to be with us for very long so she was determined to leave us with wonderful memories."

"Ruairi adored her," she added. "He wouldn't accept it when she died. He was quite sure she was still in the hospital having more tests. In fact I don't think he really got over her death until several years later when we met your family and he saw you."

"So that's why he was always so patient with me," Maggie used Sophie's cardigan to wipe away her own tears of sympathy.

Marie O'Connor nodded sadly. "Yes. You replaced the little sister he lost, while Mark, Peter and Andrew became the brothers I could never give him."

And that explains everything thought Maggie despondently as she followed the older woman into the hotel suite. Ruairi really does think of me as a little sister after all; it's just that until now I never knew it.

* * *

The children abandoned Ruairi and Maggie as soon as Mrs. O'Connor produced the room service menu and told them that as soon as they had chosen what they wanted for their supper she would telephone the hotel kitchen to order it. After much deliberation and a very detailed conversation about whether the hotel chef knew how to make proper cheese sandwiches, they placed their order, and then the three of them settled down in front of the television to watch a children's program.

Relegated to second best, Maggie wandered out onto the balcony to look at the view she had only glimpsed through the dusk on the previous evening. Below her a long rolling lawn ended at the river bank where a few hotel guests were still stretched out on recliners, making the most of the late afternoon sun. Further off a flotilla of ducks made its way upstream skillfully avoiding the boats that were drifting slowly back to their moorings. Weeping willows trailed branches in the water while cow parsley and marsh marigold softened the edges of the river and a few majestic horse chestnut trees on the far bank added a dramatic backdrop.

Ruairi joined her and handed her a long glass clinking with ice cubes. "Orange and cranberry juice with soda," he told her. "I thought you might say it was too early for wine."

"You thought right," she smiled her thanks as she sipped her drink. "With two small girls to get to bed I need all my wits about me."

"Not something you need to worry about for a while," he gestured towards the open doors of the balcony behind them. "Mum is in her absolute element. Nothing that we do on this holiday will be as good as having Sophie and Amy all to herself for an hour or two."

"Well all help is gratefully accepted," Maggie laughed. Then she grew serious.

"Your Mum just told me that she once lost a baby, a little girl."

"Yes, Colleen. I was very small, three or four I think. I don't really remember much about her."

"But she told me you doted on her."

He shook his head. "Perhaps I did but I soon forgot. I was barely more than a baby myself. I know we moved house quite soon after she died although I barely remember doing that either, but I do remember having to go to a new school."

"And that's where you met Mark and then Peter and Andrew."

He smiled down at her. "Yes. And later on I met you too."

"Your Mum says you didn't really get over your sister's death until you met me. She says I sort of replaced her in your mind."

Maggie wanted to get it out in the open, wanted to hear Ruairi tell her how it had all happened, how she had become his surrogate sister, and how he still thought of her in that way. She wanted him to say the words that would kill the hope that kept bubbling up inside her every time he touched her. She wanted him to say something that would stop her wanting him. He didn't though.

"Well that's something else that I must have forgotten too," he said, his voice unexpectedly sharp and dismissive as he took her empty glass and turned away.

He hadn't meant to snap at her but he didn't want to talk about the past. He didn't want to talk about his childhood, or about his schooldays, and he certainly didn't want to talk about the little girl who was supposed to have replaced his sister because whatever had happened when they were children, he certainly didn't have any brotherly thoughts about her now. Quite the opposite in fact! Spending so much time with her doing ordinary family things, and, although he was trying hard to forget it, holding her in his arms while she cried her heart out for June and the baby, was slowly destroying him.

* * *

Maggie turned back to the view and gazed sightlessly at the river. Ruairi's abrupt manner had startled her. Was he fed up with her? He had been so patient all day, with her and with the children. He had done everything he could to keep them entertained without once forgetting about the heartache that Mark and June were facing. Then he had taken her to the hospital when she couldn't stand the suspense any longer and, when the news was good, had been as relieved as she was. And never once during all that time had she thought about the holiday he was meant to be having and wondered whether he'd had to cancel plans of his own so he could take care of them.

Behind her the children were laughing at something on the television and then she heard Mrs. O'Connor's soft voice as she answered a knock on the door. Their tea must have arrived. She ought to go in and supervise. Then she remembered the delight on Marie O'Connor's face when she first saw the children in the elevator, and what Ruairi had just said about his mother being in her element, and she knew she had to leave them to it.

Whether she liked it or not she was going to have to stay out on the balcony for a little longer and pretend she was enjoying the view, even though she could barely see it through the blur of tears that kept leaking into her eyes. And she was going to have to pretend Ruairi was enjoying everything too; that he wasn't just being helpful because of a sense of obligation, a last link to a friendship that had faded years ago and would never have been renewed if it hadn't been for the fact that her parent's ruby wedding celebration had coincided with one of his infrequent visits home.

She also had to forget the sharpness in his voice as he left the balcony, ignore the one lapse that had shown her a glimpse of the boredom he must be feeling. After all, considering the life he was used to, it was a miracle he had managed to keep smiling all day. He had though, and if he could do it then she could too, even though her heart was slowly breaking.

Chapter Seven

Much later, after Ruairi had taken her and the children home and carried a very sleepy Amy upstairs to where Maggie was running a bath while Sophie searched for their pajamas, he offered to collect a takeaway meal while she finished putting both girls to bed.

Maggie gritted her teeth as she shook her head. No way was she going to spend the evening with him, not now it was clear to her that he was just looking after her and the children in the same way he was looking after his mother. She wasn't going to be beholden to his sense of duty for another minute, so there was a sharp edge to her own voice once she had it under control sufficiently to reply.

"No thanks. You've already done more than enough for us. Go back to the hotel and spend some time with your poor mother. After all you're meant to be giving her a holiday. I'm just going to clear up here and then have an early night. The fresh air has worn me out."

If he noticed the change in her tone of voice, he ignored it. Instead he gave her a doubtful look. "Are you sure? It's a long time since we ate that pizza."

"I'm absolutely sure. Besides, I expect Mark will arrive home soon, so I'll just wait for him to get here and then cook something for both of us."

He disentangled Amy from around his neck and passed her over. "In that case I'll go, but I'll be back in the morning," he added as both children started to protest. "And if you're good and go to sleep quickly then maybe we can do something nice again tomorrow. Perhaps we could go swimming or something."

Sophie and Amy beamed at him, hero worship shining out from their eyes as they sat at either end of the bath. Maggie felt like screaming at the unfairness of it all. Just who did he think he was suggesting treats for the children? It wasn't his job to look after them. It was hers, and as far as she was concerned he was taking his pseudo uncle role just a bit too seriously. Besides, the thought of spending a single moment in a swimming pool with him was something she didn't want to contemplate. Coping with him fully dressed was quite enough. She didn't want an intimate view of the long lean muscles that were hidden beneath his clothes, nor did she want to know whether the rest of his body was tanned to the same warm color as his face.

She was going to refuse and if it hurt his feelings, well too bad. She needed a plausible reason though, something that would stack up with Mark and June when the children told them she had refused to take them swimming because, if she was sure of one thing, it was that they would tell them. That was what children did. She cast around for something that would keep Sophie and Amy happy because she wasn't going to upset them just because she was in the middle of a stupid emotional crisis.

She had a sudden brainwave. "I'm not sure about the swimming," she said. "But I know what they would like. They would like you to bring your Mum with you tomorrow, and besides I'd enjoy spending some more time with her too." She had to speak loudly to make her voice heard above Sophie and Amy's squeals of excitement.

"That's if she doesn't have any other plans of course," she added, crossing her fingers under the soapy water as she started to wash her nieces.

"What a great idea. Thanks Maggie. I'll suggest it to her. She was talking about meeting up with some old friends but I don't think it's a definite arrangement." Ruairi's response was warm and enthusiastic.

Far too enthusiastic as far as Maggie was concerned because it confirmed what she already knew, that he would be only too glad to have someone else to take over the onerous chore of helping out with her and the children. In fact she'd probably done him a favor by suggesting it because now he knew his mother would be happy and busy too, which would be one more item ticked off on his duty agenda. He would probably deliver Mrs. O'Connor tomorrow and then suddenly remember something else he had to do and leave them to it.

Everything clear in her own mind, she gave him a small, cool smile, satisfied she had regained control of the situation. If he didn't leave voluntarily tomorrow then she would make sure he felt so outnumbered that he would be glad to escape to something more macho, like meeting up with male friends, or indulging in extreme sports or something. She was quite sure that whatever he did in his leisure time involved an adrenaline kick. After all nobody who looked like Ruairi O'Connor and led the life he did would choose to spend his time with two little girls, his ageing mother, and an emotionally challenged primary school teacher.

She remained in control as he returned her smile, pushing all thoughts of how kind he had actually been to her right out of her mind. And she would have managed to maintain her cool demeanor if he hadn't bent down and kissed the children goodnight and then angled his face to hers, smiled deep into her eyes, and kissed her cheek.

"Until tomorrow then," he said.

"Until tomorrow," she agreed, hoping he hadn't noticed a sudden shakiness in her voice, and then she kept her back towards the bathroom door so she wouldn't have to watch him walk away. Time enough for that when he goes for good, she told herself, pressing her fingers to where his kiss lingered on her cheek.

* * *

As Maggie had anticipated, Mark arrived home mid-evening, tired and disheveled but much happier and very talkative.

"He's coming out of the incubator tomorrow," he told her. "And then June will be able to feed him. The doc says that because he's such a good weight, and really strong, he's making a faster recovery than they anticipated. He is pretty sure everything is going to be fine…"

Maggie let him talk on, only half listening as she busied herself in the kitchen, determined to get some proper food into him now he could eat without worrying about his new son. As she weighed out pasta and then chopped garlic and tomatoes, her mind made its inevitable circle back to Ruairi.

How would he have reacted if it had been his son? Did he even want a son? Despite being sure he was just sticking around out of a sense of duty, she had to acknowledge he was good with children, even seemed to like them. The feeling appeared to be mutual too, if Sophie and Amy were anything to go by. They had hung onto his hands chattering nineteen-to-the-dozen as they walked along, and they had clambered willingly up onto his shoulders whenever they got the chance.

She was draining the pasta when she suddenly remembered Johanna, the tall, slim, blonde who was shortly to fly in from New Zealand. She put the saucepan down with a bang. How could she have forgotten her? It was obvious she was the person Ruairi thought of when he thought about his future; why else would he have gone to so much trouble to find her an apartment? Johanna had to be the woman who would eventually give him children and turn him into a family man instead of a rover.

"Mark…food's on the table," she deliberately pushed the painful thoughts of Ruairi and Johanna to the back of her mind as she called to her brother, who, after pouring out all his hopes and fears to her, had taken himself off to the study to telephone the rest of the family.

He came when she called him even though the phone was still clamped to his ear. "I promise you everything's fine," he was saying. "No! No! You certainly do not need to return home. Maggie has everything under control and Ruairi is helping out too, and Mrs. O'Connor. Everything is fine Mum. Just enjoy the cruise and tell Dad to order some champagne so you can both wet your new grandson's head."

He grinned at Maggie as he cut the connection. "Thank goodness I was able to give her good news. I don't want to think about what she might have done if the baby was really sick."

"Me neither," Maggie placed a bowl of pasta in front of him as well as a small dish of grated Parmesan cheese.

"Thanks sis, this looks great," he tucked in hungrily. Then he looked at her. "Aren't you having some too?"

"No...I'm not...I mean I ate earlier," Maggie stretched the truth to breaking point because she had no intention of telling him she wasn't hungry and that she didn't ever expect to feel hungry again, at least not while Ruairi O'Connor was anywhere near the vicinity of her heart.

* * *

When Maggie awoke the following morning she discovered Amy and rabbit had already joined her while Sophie was rooting through the pile of books she had left on the floor beside the bed the previous day.

"More stories," demanded Amy as soon as she opened her eyes.

"More stories," agreed Maggie, glad to be too occupied to worry about how she was going to cope with having to spend at least part of another day with Ruairi. She'd fallen asleep thinking about him and although she couldn't remember the detail, she knew he'd invaded her dreams. Consequently she hadn't slept well, and now she felt tired and stiff. One of her legs cramped as she stretched and she rubbed it hard. Then she settled down with the children to read the stories Sophie had chosen.

Mark came into the bedroom sometime later carrying a mug of tea. He laughed when he saw the three of them snuggled together, the little girls wide-eyed as they listened to Maggie using different voices for the various characters in the story she was reading.

"Look at you. I'm not sure who is enjoying it the most. It's difficult to believe you are the grown up Maggie. A good job Ruairi can't see you now or he might think he has three children to look after."

And that just about sums it up thought Maggie gloomily as she reached for her mug of tea. Ruairi does think he has three children to look after, that's why he is being so long suffering. He's being Uncle Ruairi to the three of us.

* * *

"Are you nearly ready Mum?" Ruairi tried not to let his irritation show as he waited for his mother to collect her handbag and summer jacket. After all there was no deadline. They weren't in any sort of hurry, so why the impatience? It was Maggie of course. He wanted to see her again, and as soon as possible, and he couldn't remember ever feeling this way about anyone before.

He wanted some time alone with her too. He wanted to really get to know her again, to understand the grown up Maggie. Maybe if he did that then he would get things in perspective and break the spell she seemed to have cast over him. The problem was getting some time alone with her. There was always someone else around and because of the way things were with June and the baby it didn't look as if that was going to change any time soon.

He opened the door as his mother finally announced she was ready and led the way into the corridor. He glanced down at her. She looked so happy that he felt a bit ashamed it had taken Maggie to suggest she join them for the day; Maggie to realize how much she had enjoyed seeing the children at the hotel yesterday and follow it up. He would have carried on believing her when she told him she had plans to meet up with all her old friends and that he should get on with his own life while she enjoyed her holiday in her own way. Her obvious delight when he had passed on Maggie's invitation, and the speed at which she had cancelled a proposed visit to a former neighbor so she could join them, had made him think long and hard, however. So had the newly stirred memory of his long dead sister.

Although he barely remembered Colleen, he could remember his mother being sad for what had seemed to be a very long time. He'd always known, too, that his parents would have liked more children but that for some reason they couldn't have them. Now he realized it was why they'd always kept an open house for all his friends. He recalled his childhood as they made their way to the elevator and remembered a house bursting at the seams with other people's children as his parents did their best to make up for the fact that he was an only child. The memory made him realize how selfish he had become. Why had he not seen how sad his mother's life was now she was alone? All she had were memories, and a son who rarely visited. No grandchildren, no extended family. No wonder she wanted to spend time with Sophie and Amy.

He followed her into the elevator and listened to her plans for the day while it took them down to the underground car park. Nodding and smiling he directed her towards his hire car, half wishing he wasn't also nursing an ulterior motive. Although he was ashamed he hadn't given his mother more than a passing thought while he spent his time with Maggie, now that she was included he hoped she'd look after the children for a couple of hours so he could take Maggie out to lunch. Not that he had any intention of letting her or Maggie know his plans. He was just going to trust his instincts and count on his mother making the suggestion herself.

He wasn't sure why he was being so reticent. After all, his mother would be happy to oblige if he asked her outright. She would be thrilled if he showed an interest in Maggie too, except, of course, that was the problem. A couple of dates with Maggie and she would be talking weddings and bridesmaids. It had always been the same. So desperate was she for grandchildren that ever since he could remember she had honed in on any girl he mentioned, so she certainly wasn't going to make an exception of Maggie.

He unlocked the car and settled her into the passenger seat before walking round to the driver's door. He opened it with a sigh. No! There was no way he was going to talk to her about Maggie, not when he had no intention of doing anything more than take her out to lunch. They were old friends catching up and that was all there was to it.

Chapter Eight

The morning passed without incident. Using some bits and pieces of wood he found in Mark's garage, Ruairi busied himself building a den for the children. They pretended to help while running around the garden in a frenzy of excitement and shouting out random orders.

"It must be big," Amy yelled.

"With a proper roof and stairs and everything," said Sophie as she paused for breath.

Ruairi reappeared from inside the slightly lopsided construction. "I don't think I can quite manage that," he told her with a chuckle of amusement. "But I might manage a window and a door."

"Can we live in it?" asked Amy.

Sophie was scathing. "Course not 'cos there aren't any bedrooms but I 'spect we'll eat dinner there," she said, with a hopeful look in Maggie's direction.

Maggie, who was trying to keep Ruairi out of her line of vision as much as possible, was sitting on a garden chair chatting to Mrs.

O'Connor over a cup of coffee so she didn't hear Sophie's request.

Ruairi did though and he straightened up thoughtfully. "How about it?" he said, walking over to where Maggie and his mother were sitting.

"How about what?" Her conversation interrupted, Maggie glared up at him from behind her sunglasses, wishing for the umpteenth time that the black denims and T-shirt he was wearing didn't have the effect of making him look more devastating than usual.

"Sophie thinks the den will be a good place to eat her lunch once it's finished."

Mrs. O'Connor leapt in before Maggie could speak. "What a good idea. Would she be wanting a picnic perhaps?"

"Yes! Yes! We can have a den picnic…a den picnic…a den picnic," Sophie chanted as she fixed her aunt with a fierce stare that dared her to disagree.

Maggie laughed. "Of course you can but you'll have to help me get it ready. Let's go and see what's in the fridge."

Mrs. O'Connor joined them as they made their way back to the house. "I'm sorry my dear. I shouldn't have jumped in like that without checking with you. It's just that it's so like old times having children around, making things with them, seeing them enjoy themselves, that I didn't stop to think."

Maggie, hearing the wistful note in her voice, shook her head. "It's not a problem. I would have said yes anyway. I remember how much I loved having picnics in the playhouse that...." her voice trailed away as she remembered it was Ruairi who had built her a den when she was a child.

Marie O'Connor chuckled as she reminisced. "He hasn't really changed has he, despite all his travelling. Look at him! Just as determined to get it right now as he was years ago when he was building things for you, although he's a bit better at it this time around."

Forced to stand still and look at what Ruairi had managed to concoct with a few pieces of wood, some nails, and some flattened cardboard boxes, Maggie had to agree. Not that the wonkiness of her own childhood den and the way it had leaned precariously against the fence had ever bothered her. She'd thought it was absolutely perfect the same as she'd thought Ruairi was absolutely perfect. She wondered about it now though. Had she hero-worshipped him just because he'd been so different from her brothers, or had there been more to it than that? Could a small girl fall in love? Had the hours they'd spent together when she was a child sowed the seeds of the feelings she had for him now?

"This feels a bit like old times," his job finished, Ruairi joined them, interrupting her thoughts. He was holding Mark's toolbox. He looked at Maggie. "Do you remember?"

"Of course I do, except I'm sure my den was a bit more substantial than this one because although it got more and more battered every winter, it still lasted for several years," she couldn't stop the smile the memory triggered despite her uncomfortable thoughts.

"That's because I didn't have to rely on cardboard for the walls! This one will be history as soon as it rains, whereas your Dad gave me the run of his tool shed, something he regretted when he realized I'd used nearly all his spare pieces of wood."

"And you found an old tarpaulin in the attic too," his mother reminded him. "Somehow you managed to drag it down the ladder and then you fixed it over everything. You said it would make it more weatherproof. I remember Maggie being so excited about it."

"Me too!" Ruairi agreed with a sly look at Maggie. "And then she took to hiding there whenever she was in trouble, which just goes to show she had no imagination whatsoever because after the first couple of times everyone always knew exactly where to find her."

"Excuse me, both of you, but I am here you know," Maggie reminded them. "Besides, I never was in any sort of trouble."

Such a blatant denial made them all laugh and by the time they reached the kitchen, despite Maggie's determination to keep Ruairi at arm's length, the warm memories of the past had enveloped them all, so when Marie O'Connor suggested they went out to lunch while she and the children had a picnic in the den, Maggie couldn't find the words to refuse her kind offer.

* * *

Trying very hard not to look too pleased with himself, Ruairi slotted his car into the one remaining space in the car park and killed the engine. At last he could spend some time alone with Maggie. Admittedly it was only for a couple of hours at the local inn, but it was better than nothing. Apart from anything else, he hoped it would be long enough to find out why she had waxed so hot and cold this morning: cool and distant one minute and friendly the next. And long enough, too, to ask her about her travel plans, where she was going and for how long. Then, if there was any time left, he was going to talk about his next assignment. If he put enough enthusiasm into telling her about his forthcoming trip to Mexico then perhaps he would manage to persuade himself it was a good idea and start to look forward to it, instead of spending all his time wondering why he wanted to put so many miles between himself and the people he loved.

Pushing away such confusing thoughts he turned towards her with a teasing smile. "Are you sure no one in your family knows we're here?"

"Absolutely positive unless they have extrasensory perception," she said, a dimple shadowing her cheek as she laughed.

They walked across the car park in a companionable silence that continued until a waitress ushered them to a table near an open window. Ruairi ordered a drink for each of them and then directed Maggie's attention to the menu.

Drinks delivered and their order taken, he raised his glass. "Here's to an uninterrupted lunch!"

Right on cue, his cell phone rang. With a wry smile of apology he looked at the number and then answered it.

"Jo!" his voice was warm and welcoming. Then there was a long silence as he listened, his face full of surprise and pleasure. Finally he answered.

"Tomorrow you say, at three o'clock. Right, I'll be there."

There was another pause and then he answered what was obviously a question.

"No, nothing has changed since we spoke earlier. The apartment is all fixed. I'll ring the agent and let her know I need to collect the key tomorrow morning instead of Friday. It won't be a problem, and she already knows to contact you about the tenancy agreement as soon as you've moved in. It's a great apartment. Maggie helped me find it and I'm sure she'll help with the groceries too."

A further pause, then he chuckled. "No, no, nothing like that! Maggie's just an old friend from way back."

He smiled across the table at Maggie as he spoke. And Maggie, her mellow mood dispersed first by the phone call, and then by his casual dismissal of her place in his life, dredged up every ounce of will power she possessed and forced the muscles of her face into an answering smile.

* * *

"That was Jo," he informed her quite unnecessarily as he slipped his cell phone back into his pocket. "She's arriving tomorrow afternoon, a couple of days earlier than I expected."

"And she wants us to do some shopping for her."

"Mmm, not much. Just bread, milk, coffee…things like that. We could pick it up on our way back to Mark's house. She says hello, by the way. She's looking forward to meeting you."

Maggie's stoicism didn't stretch to saying she was looking forward to meeting Jo too, so instead she hid herself behind her glass of tomato juice and wondered how the other girl had managed such perfect timing. At a stroke the phone call had destroyed her appetite as well as her equanimity. With an effort she tuned back in to Ruairi. He was still talking about Jo.

"You'll like her," he was saying. "In fact I hope the two of you will be friends because she doesn't know many people in the UK, so she could do with some help while she settles in. You know, stuff about doctors and dentists and things like that."

The waitress interrupted with their food. But although she picked up her knife and fork, Maggie did little more than push the food around her plate. All she could think about was that on top of everything else she was now expected to be best friends with the unknown Johanna. First Mrs. O'Connor had asked her to find out what was wrong with Ruairi, and now he wanted her to look after his girlfriend.

Well she'd solved Mrs. O'Connor's problem anyway, because now she'd seen him light up when he talked to Jo, Ruairi's problem was obvious. Anyone with half a brain could tell that he was missing her. As soon as she arrived the sadness his mother was worried about would disappear and everyone except Maggie would be happy. As for being friends with tall, blonde, blue-eyed Jo…well she wasn't even going to think about that.

Ruairi continued to talk about her as he started to attack the steak he had ordered. "She asked if you were coming to the airport to meet her," he said.

And why would I want to trail out to the airport to meet a complete stranger and then stand by and watch her kiss you, thought Maggie mutinously. Clamping her mouth tight shut so she didn't say it out loud, she gave a non-committal shrug. Bad mistake because it wasn't enough to curb his enthusiasm.

"I know! We can all go. There's hardly any traffic at that time of day and if we get there early enough we can take the girls into the observation area so they can see the planes landing and taking off. They'll love it, and Jo will love them."

* * *

By the time they returned to the house laden with Johanna's shopping, everything had been agreed. Ruairi was to collect Maggie and the girls after he had picked up the key from the estate agent. Then the four of them would go to the new apartment to offload the bags of food and pack everything away in the empty cupboards and fridge. After that they would drive to the airport where they would climb up to the observation area to watch for Jo's plane.

Maggie had reluctantly agreed to everything Ruairi suggested because she couldn't think of a single reason not to as far as everyone else was concerned. He wanted her to meet Jo. Jo wanted to meet her. And she knew he was right about the girls too. They would find driving to the airport an adventure, and they would love watching the planes. They hadn't done much travelling in their short lives, so everything would be a novelty. And it would be a novelty that Ruairi's enthusiasm would make doubly exciting, so how could she possibly deny them. Besides, she had to meet Johanna sometime, so why not tomorrow, as soon as she arrived. She would just get it over and done with so that she could get on with her life without spending every spare minute thinking about the pair of them. With any luck, her heart would stop jumping sideways every time she looked at Ruairi and settle back into its normal rhythm once she actually saw him kissing another woman.

She cleared a space in the fridge for Johanna's two-liter bottle of milk and carton of orange juice and then stacked the rest of the shopping onto the kitchen counter while Ruairi went to find Sophie and Amy. She could hear them greeting him, their excitement at a decibel level that made it sound as if he had just returned from the North Pole. Determined to take herself in hand, she filled the kettle and pulled mugs from the cupboard. She would make some tea and when she took it into the garden she would pretend everything was fine, that she had enjoyed lunch and that she couldn't wait to meet the unknown Jo.

* * *

Sophie and Amy ran pell-mell across the lawn when they saw her.

"Come and see what Granny Connor has done to our den," they pleaded, pulling at her cotton skirt to hurry her along.

"Their idea, not Mum's...the Granny Connor thing," Ruairi told her with a grin as he rescued the tray of mugs before she dropped them. "Not that she minds of course!"

The smile that Maggie had already pasted on her face became more genuine. She knew how much Mrs. O'Connor would love being called Granny Connor. Knew how much she would actually love to have grandchildren of her own. She gave an inward sigh as she followed the children. Well perhaps she would be lucky soon. Perhaps Johanna would oblige.

Chapter Nine

The girls were ready and waiting for Ruairi by eight-thirty the following morning despite being told by Maggie that it was far too early. They peered expectantly through the window and commented on everyone who passed by as they watched for his car. Maggie took advantage of their preoccupation to sort the laundry, make the beds, and do some basic housekeeping. The time she was spending with Ruairi was interfering with her chores as well as her heart, and although she knew June would be grateful for whatever she did, she also knew her sister-in-law liked to keep a tidy house. Besides, she would have her work cut out for her over the next few months with a new baby and two energetic little girls, so the least Maggie could do was to try to keep things on schedule.

"Bye sis," Mark called out to her as the front door banged behind him. He was off to the hospital again although he had promised to be back for Sophie and Amy's bedtime.

She didn't bother to reply knowing he would already be halfway to his car. He had been doing everything on the run since the baby arrived and she hoped he would slow down soon and try to relax before June came home with their new son. For the first time she wished her mother was here instead of thousands of miles away because she would be able to make him see sense whereas Maggie had no influence at all. She knew he was grateful for everything she was doing but she also knew he wouldn't thank her for suggesting he needed to sleep a bit more, or maybe spend more time with Sophie and Amy. It would be the same old reaction as always; he would just tell her she didn't know what she was talking about because she hadn't been there herself, so who was she to give him advice.

She finished unloading the washing machine and carried the full laundry basket into the garden. As she started to peg the wet clothes onto the washing line her thoughts were still on her brother, but by the time she bent down to pull another small garment from the pile of wet laundry she was thinking about Ruairi again, as she had been doing on and off for most of the morning.

He would be ringing the doorbell in less than an hour and by then she would have to be cool, calm and collected, not the wreck she had been ever since yesterday's lunch.

From the beginning she had known it would be a mistake to spend too much time alone with him but until yesterday she hadn't realized quite how much. Of course it had started off badly with Johanna's phone call, and then Ruairi had spent far too much time talking about her. Far,

104

far too much time, so that in the end instead of just disliking Johanna she had positively hated her, or at least the thought of her. But then, as if he had suddenly realized how she felt, he had switched his attention to her, and for the rest of the meal he had probed and questioned until, without really meaning to, she had told him about her plans to travel to a country where teachers were in short supply

Over the remains of salad and then coffee they had discussed the different countries she was considering, the children she would like to teach. Ruairi had been to all of them and she had been grateful for his advice even though she knew it was the first step in a long and lonely journey away from him.

Then they had talked about his work and as he described the utter peace and isolation of the beach where he had spent the past few months filming a breeding colony of New Zealand fur seals and their pups for a TV production company, she could almost see it. He'd told her about his next assignment too, about how he was going to Mexico to film the annual migration of monarch butterflies. He'd said it was something he'd wanted to do for a very long time, and as she'd listened to his description she understood why.

"They are such beautiful insects Maggie, as well as one of the most fascinating. Did you know that huge numbers of them migrate up to two and a half thousand miles to escape the cold North American weather? Not all of them though. The ones who migrate are fourth generation butterflies. That's because the first three generations of every year only live for about six weeks, just long enough to reproduce, whereas the fourth and final generation of their annual breeding cycle lives for around eight months. This is so they can migrate to a warmer climate, hibernate, and that start a new first generation in the spring when they return."

"That's not all either. When they migrate, whether it's to Mexico or to Southern California, they always hibernate in the same trees even though none of them have ever been there before. In Mexico it's the oyamel fir trees and in California they settle in the coastal eucalyptus groves. I wish you could see the migration. The trees are absolutely covered in butterflies and, when they first arrive, the ground is too. Everywhere is just a fluttering kaleidoscope of orange and black and when the sun shines on them, well it's just magical. I can't wait to see it again and, this time, to actually get paid for filming it too."

By the time they had finished their meal Maggie was completely enthralled. She wanted to learn more about the extraordinary life he lived, the places he had visited, the wildlife he had seen up close and personal. She wanted to know if it was ever dangerous, what he enjoyed the most, what he still wanted to do, but by then it was time to do Johanna's shopping, so she had been left with too many unanswered questions and no time to ask them.

Then, soon after they had returned to the house, while her mind was still seething with everything he had told her, Mark had come home to spend his promised quality time with his daughters, except that Sophie and Amy weren't interested. They were far too busy playing house with Mrs. O'Connor to even notice him, so he invited Ruairi to join him in front of the TV so they could catch up on the latest sporting results while they drank cans of beer. And there they stayed until Mrs. O'Connor gathered up her belongings and declared it was time to return to the hotel.

The girls danced attendance all the way down the path to the garden gate, pestering Ruairi with questions about the next day's big adventure. Mark had come too and given Mrs. O'Connor a hug as he thanked her for looking after Sophie and Amy. Watching them all, Maggie suddenly felt superfluous; certain that if she opened the gate and walked away nobody would even notice her go. She was just good old Maggie. Fine for filling in the gaps but not exciting enough to feature very highly in the wider scheme of things. She hadn't thought up exciting projects like Ruairi, or turned a rickety cardboard den into a magical house like Mrs. O'Connor. She wasn't even a worthy companion for Mark when he wanted to talk sport. He needed Ruairi for that. And on top of everything, listening to Ruairi talk about his adventures at lunchtime had made her realize how very constrained and narrow her own life was and it wasn't a comfortable thought. As soon as June was back at home she was going to have to take herself in hand and do something about her life instead of just talking about it.

Oh for goodness sake stop feeling so sorry for yourself she told herself crossly as she kissed Mrs. O'Connor goodbye and promised to see her again very soon. Then she held onto Sophie and Amy to stop them running out into the street while Ruairi, having said goodbye to Mark, bent to kiss them. When he straightened up he looked directly at her.

"Are you okay?" he asked quietly, a slight frown between his eyes.

"Why wouldn't I be?" She wished his eyes weren't so changeable. There were specks of gold in there, and green, and yellow, all circled by a dark ring like the eyes of the big cats he'd told her he sometimes filmed. And they were just as piercing too. For one stupid moment she was almost persuaded he could see inside her head and that he knew exactly what she was thinking, then commonsense took over and she hastily swung a fidgeting Amy up onto her hip, anxious to distract him.

"I don't know," he admitted. "You just seem…well a bit quiet. You are okay with tomorrow's plans aren't you?"

"Of course I am," she lied. Then she shifted Amy from her hip to her stomach, effectively making a barrier between her and Ruairi because she wasn't going to let him kiss her cheek the same as he had just done to Sophie and Amy. Recognizing the preliminary move, she was determined to stop him. To be put on an equal footing with her nieces while he lusted after the soon to be with them Johanna...well she could bear almost anything but that.

* * *

A loud wail from Amy brought her back to the here and now. Abandoning the rest of the laundry she hurried indoors. It was only a bumped knee, the result of a tumble from the chair near the window where she was waiting for Ruairi, but by the time Maggie had kissed it better, persuaded Sophie to run upstairs to collect sweaters for both of them, and checked her own hair in the hall mirror, Ruairi had arrived.

With no time to gather her thoughts, Maggie shepherded both girls through the front door, slung June's capacious shopping bag over her shoulder, picked up the plastic bags containing the rest of Johanna's groceries, and locked up the house. By the time she reached the car Ruairi had strapped both girls into their seats and was waiting for her beside the passenger door.

He looked, if anything, more devastating than usual even though he was only wearing denims and an olive green sweatshirt. It's because it matches his eyes, she told herself. Then she remembered it was all for Jo anyway and tried not to let her misery show as she settled herself into the passenger seat and deliberately didn't watch him walk around the car to the driver's door.

* * *

Ruairi frowned. There was definitely something wrong, he just couldn't figure out what. She was smiling in all the right places, saying the right things and yet…his mind went back over the years to the younger Maggie. Even then he'd always known when she wasn't happy although getting it out of her had never been easy. Too used to being teased by her brothers she could never quite believe he was prepared to take her seriously, and it had often taken him days to get past her armor of self-protection. Nor had he ever really understood why it was so important to him to know what she was thinking, not until now.

He glanced sideways at her as he started the engine. She looked lost somehow, diminished. Something had changed and she was a different Maggie from the laughing girl he'd met at her parent's ruby wedding celebration. Then she had been full of life, her grey eyes alight with humor, those fascinating dimples constantly shadowing her cheeks as she chattered away. She'd been funny too, bursting into peals of laughter every time she remembered something funny from her childhood.

Her smile, the way they had caught up on ten years of history without a pause, had soothed him in a way that nothing else had, not the genuine welcome from the rest of the Silver family nor their exclamations of interest when he'd answered questions about his work. After so many years he was used to that, in the same way he was used to expressions of astonishment and admiration when he was asked about some of his scarier wildlife encounters. He was even used to the invitation he'd seen in the eyes of some of the women at the party although he hadn't taken them seriously. He never did nowadays although years ago, when he was much younger, he hadn't always been so circumspect. Nowadays, however, he knew the look for what it was. It wasn't really about him. It was a fascination with the unknown, a wish, however vicariously, to experience a life that from the outside seemed exotic but from the inside, if only they knew, was often anything but.

Maggie hadn't been like that though. Her welcome had been for him, not for who he had become. She hadn't acted impressed. He wasn't even sure she'd seen any of the TV documentaries he'd filmed. If she had then she hadn't mentioned them. She'd just been happy to see him. To her he was Ruairi, not someone with a growing reputation in the world of wildlife documentary, and once they'd got past that silly crush thing she'd had on him when she was a child, it had been fine...well it would have been fine if he hadn't found himself falling for her big time. And that was why he was in such a dilemma now because although he hated to see her unhappy he wasn't sure he could do anything about it, not when he was doing everything he could to avoid intimacy while trying as hard as he could to showcase the cheery, avuncular image that seemed just about the safest thing he could manage.

Not that any of it mattered right now because by the time they reached the end of the road Sophie and Amy had taken over and for the rest of the journey both he and Maggie were too occupied with answering questions, acting as arbitrators when arguments got out of hand and, as they approached the airport, offering their services as tour guides, for either of them to worry about their own personal dilemmas.

* * *

As Ruairi had predicted, the sight of aircraft approaching and leaving the runways transfixed both children and it was all Maggie could do to persuade them to take a little time off for lunch. Then, full of fish fingers and chips, and each clutching a small teddy bear dressed in a pilot's cap and jacket that had been bought for them by Ruairi, they clamored to be allowed back into the observation area to watch for Johanna's plane.

Following them as they raced towards the lift, Ruairi gave Maggie a wry smile. "They're pretty full on aren't they?"

She gave him what looked like the first genuine Maggie smile of the day. "Try a class of twenty five-year-olds, then you'll know what full on really means!"

"Twenty! Really?" The look of horror on his face filled her with amusement as she nodded.

"In that case give me a herd of rampaging elephants any day!"

He was still chuckling as they pushed their way through the doors leading to the open-air observation area. Then it was back to answering questions, pointing out the different insignias on the tail fins of the planes, and waiting for Johanna.

At three o clock Ruairi pointed upwards. 'There it is! That's Jo's plane." He lifted Amy up and gently tilted her face in the right direction.

"How do you know?" Sophie demanded.

He shrugged. "I just do."

"Ruairi has done a lot of travelling," Maggie explained, wishing she could shoot the plane down before it landed. "He's been to lots of different countries all over the world."

"Even as far as Cornwall?" asked Amy.

"Even as far as Cornwall," she agreed solemnly, knowing this was the furthest Amy had travelled in her three years.

"He's been further than that silly," said the all-knowing Sophie. "He's been to countries where there are elephants and tigers and…and…and other things too."

113

"So have I," came the indignant rejoinder as her sister remembered her one visit to a zoo.

Trying very hard not to laugh, Maggie explained the difference and then, all too soon, Ruairi was looking at his watch and telling them it was time to go and meet Johanna.

"Her plane will have landed by now," he explained. "And we must be there waiting for her once she has collected her suitcase or she'll think we've forgotten to meet her."

Agreeing that this was indeed a necessity, Sophie led the way while Amy, suddenly shy at the thought of meeting a stranger, clutched pink rabbit to her chest with one hand and clung onto Maggie with the other.

* * *

I so do not want to be here. The words were like a mantra in Maggie's head. They had been waiting for Johanna for quite a while now. Families had arrived and been greeted by grandparents, aunts, uncles, friends. Tired looking businessmen and women whose trips had been too short for them to adjust to their jetlag had rushed by laden down with executive briefcases, lap tops and identical luggage. Couples, mostly suntanned, some young, some older, had all hurried onto the main concourse searching for loved ones, or to find a taxi. Now the doors through to the Baggage Claim remained mostly closed, only opening occasionally for a final straggler or two.

Maggie began to feel hopeful. Perhaps Johanna had missed the plane. Perhaps she was going to have a reprieve. Her hopes were dashed when the automatic door swished open again and another flurry of passengers came through.

"There she is," Ruairi said, the pleasure in his voice far too obvious.

"Where?" Sophie stood on tiptoe to see over the barrier while Amy clutched Maggie's hand even more tightly.

"There! That's Jo!" Ruairi pointed to a tall fair-haired woman pushing a laden trolley. She was walking towards them with a broad smile on her face.

She was everything Maggie had expected her to be. Her hair was streaked blonde from the sun and she topped Maggie by a good six inches. Plus she was really lovely to look at in a healthy outdoor sort of way; all long limbs, smooth tan skin, bright blue eyes and good teeth. Everything about her was to hate except for one undeniable thing. She was very obviously pregnant.

"I'm so sorry I kept you waiting," the accent was faintly Scandinavian. "There was a mix up over the baggage. Someone nearly walked away with one of my suitcases."

Ruairi grinned at her. "When were you ever on time for anything?" he said, kissing her on both cheeks before introducing her to Maggie and the children.

She ignored his jibe as she turned to Maggie. "Am I pleased to meet you," she told her. "After nearly six months of mostly male company I am so overloaded with testosterone that when Ruairi told me that he was bringing you to the airport I burst into tears."

"That's a hormonal thing too," he teased.

"Probably true given this," she patted her swelling stomach with a smile, but there was nothing more than casual affection in her response.

Maggie immediately pushed aside the shameful thought that had flashed across her mind when Jo had first appeared. This baby was nothing to do with Ruairi, anymore than Jo was. Jo was just a work colleague, a friend. She gave her a smile of welcome. The one that lit up her eyes and highlighted her dimples, the one that turned Ruairi's stomach upside down and made him forget to breathe.

He felt an overwhelming sense of relief. The old Maggie was back. He didn't know what the problem had been but whatever it was, it had gone, and she was happy again. She also seemed to like Jo. Two problems solved in less than a minute. What more could a man ask for? He perched a giggling Sophie on top of Jo's over-laden trolley and led the way to the exit.

Jo and Maggie followed behind with a suddenly much more confident Amy swinging from both their hands. He glanced back at them as he made his way across to the car park. They were deep in conversation.

Chapter Ten

"Everything has been such a rush," Jo was telling Maggie. "I didn't know I was pregnant when I set off for New Zealand. I only found out when I kept throwing up on the flight out, except that, at the time, I stupidly thought it was some sort of stomach bug. Once I realized the truth though, we had to rethink our plans."

"We?"

"Ollie and me. Ollie's my husband. We were both contracted to spend a year in New Zealand, the same as Ruairi, but although New Zealand has excellent medical facilities we both decided we wanted to come home for the birth."

She saw the question in Maggie's eyes and laughed. "England is home for both of us. I love Sweden but I left such a long time ago that it barely seems relevant to my life anymore. Now we just go there for holidays. Being back in the UK will make it much easier for my parents to fly over to visit their first grandchild too. They would never have made it to New Zealand and nor would Ollie's parents. They're all quite elderly and Ollie's Mum has poor health as well, although she's not so poorly that she isn't head-over-heels excited about this baby."

"Is a first for them too?"

Jo gave a peal of laughter as they paused to let a taxi go by and then crossed into the car park. "Far from it. They already have so many grandchildren that I've lost count. It's Ollie they're pleased about. Becoming a father, getting married even is a cause for celebration as far as they're concerned. They had long given him up as a lost cause. He was always too busy travelling the world to think about his future."

"Until he met you," Maggie's voice shook slightly. Ollie sounded just like Ruairi, and yet he'd finally met someone and fallen in love and now he seemed ready to settle down. She wanted to know how Jo had met and tamed him.

"Well if you can call almost knocking me off the side of a cliff meeting me, then yes," Jo was still laughing when they reached the car and all conversation had to stop while her luggage was loaded into the trunk. Then, with Maggie wedged in between the children's car seats in the back of the car, Jo turned her head to finish answering the question.

"It happened when I first visited New Zealand a few years ago. I had been there for a month or so when Ollie arrived. I was studying a breeding colony of cormorants that nest on some very inaccessible cliffs. He was there to film some of the other bird life and he was familiarizing himself with the site and scoping where to set up his equipment when he strayed into the one tiny bit of territory I'd declared out of bounds to the rest of the crew."

118

She smiled at the memory. "I didn't make him very welcome I'm afraid."

"From what I heard the poor man was a complete wreck for weeks," Ruairi interjected. "Apparently everyone became so fed up with him they decided to do something about it before their whole project failed."

"That is so not true," Jo protested.

He chuckled as he drove the car out of the airport and filtered onto the highway. "I seem to remember something about a romantic meal for two!"

"Oh that!"

"Yes, that! From what I heard, he'd still be in decline now if the rest of the crew hadn't made themselves scarce by going off to the nearest village for a night of socializing and leaving you two behind to mind camp. Apparently they reckoned you both just needed a bit of uninterrupted time together and they were proved right!"

His eyes met Maggie's in the driver's mirror as he spoke. It was only a fleeting glance but there was something in his expression that jolted her. She remembered how often he'd tried to carve out uninterrupted time for the two of them and how, every time, he'd been thwarted, and briefly she wondered if there was a message in his words. Then she dismissed it. She was being stupid. After all he had spent the little time they had together yesterday telling her all about his next assignment, how he was about to spend another long stretch out of the country.

Dragging her eyes away from her reflection in the driving mirror she directed them towards the passing scenery and for the rest of the journey she and the girls played word games while Jo and Ruairi chatted quietly in the front of the car.

* * *

"Like her?" Ruairi asked some time later as he pointed the car towards Mark's house and the children's tea, bath and bedtime.

"Very much," Maggie said. And she did. She really liked Jo. A lot. And not just because she was pregnant, had a husband, and had turned out to be very different from the imaginary temptress who had haunted her thoughts for the past few days.

She not only liked her, she admired her. They had talked some more when they reached the apartment, and the more she'd learned about the older woman, the more she wanted to be like her. Jo took chances. She lived an independent life. She did what she wanted to without worrying about what other people thought of her. In short, she had already done what Maggie was planning to do and travelled and worked in foreign countries, but with far less angst and far more determination.

She was looking forward to seeing her again in two days time. She'd agreed to it knowing she'd be free because it was when Mark was taking Sophie and Amy to the hospital to see June and to meet their new brother. The baby was out of the incubator now and no longer hooked up to the various machines that had been monitoring his progress, so at last he looked like a regular baby and was nearly ready to start meeting the rest of the family.

"I won't be fit for anything tomorrow," Jo had explained. "Not once the jetlag kicks in. By why don't we meet up the day after?"

Maggie had accepted with pleasure and then they'd both looked at Ruairi.

He'd shaken his head in amusement. "Don't look so worried. I know when I'm not wanted. Besides I've a few things to do of my own."

Just a throw away remark but it had jolted Maggie into realizing how much of his precious holiday time he was giving up to help out with Mark and the children and she knew she would have to say something about it. Now, with the children too worn out by the day's excitement to do more than gaze sleepily at the passing traffic, she had her chance.

"Um...you don't need to bother about us tomorrow you know...now that the baby is...Mark will be around more and...well I know you've got things to do. Although I don't want you to think that I'm not grateful for everything you have done of course...I mean..." she tailed off hopelessly. It sounded so wrong, so formal. It sounded as if she was dismissing him. Why did she keep getting it so wrong?

She risked a look in his direction. He was concentrating on the rush hour traffic and didn't immediately reply. Unable to help herself she feasted her eyes on his profile for just a moment too long, so that when he glanced across at her their eyes met and for the second time that day she thought she saw some sort of message in them. Then he turned back to the traffic. His voice, when he finally spoke, sounded just the same as it always did. Deep, warm, with that hint of underlying laughter.

"Are you trying to get rid of me Maggie Silver?"

"No! Well…not really…it's just that I…you're meant to be giving your Mum a holiday and it doesn't seem very fair to her if you spend all your time with us," her final words came out in a rush.

"Mum is so busy meeting old friends that she's barely got time to have breakfast with me," he said.

"Well what about your own friends? Surely there are people you want to see. I'm sure my brothers would love to spend more time with you for a start."

"In the evening maybe, but not during the day Maggie. Everyone is at work during the day. Besides, I've been away for too long now. Lots of the old links are broken. I don't fit any more. Nobody does once they've been away for a few years."

"Why not?"

"Lots of reasons I guess, but mainly because life has taken us in different directions. For a day or two people are welcoming, interested even, but then they want to get back to their own lives, back to familiarity. Too much time spent with someone who has travelled a lot, someone who has seen and experienced things beyond the normal reach of an annual holiday, can be unsettling. And people don't want to be unsettled."

"I never thought of it like that."

"Why should you? But you need to remember it when you start your own travels because, without meaning to, your family and friends will see your absence as a rejection of everything they hold dear and they will close ranks just a little. And each time you go away the gap between you will grow just that tiny bit bigger."

Maggie stared at him. She had had no idea. She hadn't thought beyond wanting to get away from her family's constant advice and do something different. She hadn't really considered what it might do to her family and friends. Then, while she was still digesting what he'd said, she had another thought. Was that what made Ruairi unhappy, the fact that he didn't fit any more? Not that she had actually seen his unhappiness but Mrs. O'Connor had seemed so sure. She would have another conversation with her about it before she went back to Ireland and tell her everything Ruairi had just said.

"Are you?" his question cut across her thoughts.

"Am I what?"

"Trying to get rid of me?"

She smiled at him. "I wouldn't be that unkind when you so obviously have nowhere else to go!"

He ignored her teasing sarcasm. "That's good because I have plans for tomorrow." 'What plans?"

He drew up in front of the house and smiled across at her. "You'll just have to wait and see."

* * *

And now it was tomorrow, and he was due at any moment, and Maggie felt like screaming. She'd already had three phone calls. The first one had been a check up call from her mother. Not that she was checking on the baby's progress, or June's health, she had already spoken to Mark about that. No! This was Maggie's check up call.

Had she remembered that Amy couldn't go to sleep without pink rabbit? Had she remembered that Sophie didn't like custard and that she wouldn't eat anything that was even the tiniest bit soggy? And how was she coping with the laundry? And had she changed the beds yet because it would be best if June came home to a clean house…and then there was the shopping…

Maggie had tuned out, knowing it was only her mother's anxiety talking; knowing that however much she was enjoying her cruise she was still itching to get back and take over. It had still stung though. After all, if June thought she was up to coping with the children, then her mother should too.

She was still recovering her equanimity when the phone rang again. This time it was Jenny, her brother Peter's wife, with a suggestion that they all meet together in the park for a lunchtime picnic.

"It'll do Sophie and Amy good," she had said. "Take them out of themselves; stop them missing June so much."

"I'll get back to you when Ruairi arrives. He might have made other plans," Maggie had told her, trying to keep the irritation out of her voice because she knew Jenny was only trying to help. Biting her tongue, she'd cut the call without bothering to tell her that far from missing June, the children were having the time of their lives thanks to Ruairi and Mrs. O'Connor.

Then Helen, Andrew's wife, had phoned, reissuing the same invitation; and that was when Maggie realized they were not only in cahoots with one another but that her mother had put them up to it. She sighed as she gave Helen the same reply.

She got on well with all of her sisters-in-law, although June was her favorite, probably because she treated her like a capable adult. The other two just went along with her family's assessment without question and treated her like an overgrown child, someone who was fine for babysitting and entertaining their respective broods at family gatherings, but not someone capable of managing her own life without the benefit of their advice.

She stared at her face in the mirror as she picked up her brush ready to tackle the tangle of her hair. Up until now she hadn't had any time for herself thanks to all those phone calls, Sophie and Amy's breakfast demands, and Mark's shamefaced request that she help him search for a clean shirt, then his shoes, and finally his cell phone.

She had watched him set off for work with a disbelieving shake of her head. He was spending a few hours each day at the office now that things had settled down because he wanted to save most of his paternity leave for when June brought the baby home. Idly she wondered if he was always so disorganized or whether, deep down, he was still worried about the baby despite the pediatrician's assurance that everything was fine. With no way of knowing she'd dismissed him from her thoughts and returned to the kitchen where she'd managed to gulp down a few mouthfuls of coffee and eat half a slice of toast before she was needed to referee a minor disagreement between Sophie and Amy.

Now, however, both girls were sitting quietly in front of the television watching a children's program, which meant she could take time to do her hair, put on some make up and think about the day ahead.

She felt bad about her recent behavior. She knew that believing Jo was Ruairi's girlfriend was no excuse. Jealousy was an unattractive trait, especially as Ruairi had never given her any reason to think she had a right to be jealous about him. Ever since he had come back into her life he'd treated her exactly the way she'd seen him treat Jo. To Ruairi she was no more than a good friend, someone to spend time with...except...except there had been just one or two moments, fleeting glances, the warmth of his arm as he briefly squeezed her shoulder, the way he smiled at her, that not only set her pulses racing but also made her wonder if he might feel something more for her after all. Maybe he was holding back because she had been so vehement about her plans to travel when she told him her plans, or maybe she was just deluding herself and it was her imagination. Nevertheless it was enough to make her decide to do something about it.

So what if he laughed at her? So what if she made a fool of herself? Anything would be better than just letting him disappear out of her life again without at least putting up a fight. She wasn't naïve enough to think there was only one person out there for her. It was a big world after all. But she did know that the feelings she had for Ruairi, had always had for Ruairi, were far too important to ignore.

She finished smoothing her hair into place, brushed mascara onto her eyelashes and colored her lips with a new lip-gloss. There! She was ready. If that didn't do it then nothing would. She knew she looked good. She was wearing a blue and white spotted sundress that fitted where it touched across the body and then flared out into a skirt that swirled and dipped as she moved. And it was a color that suited her. It reflected the color of her eyes and set off the burnished gloss of her hair. Satisfied with her image in the mirror, she slipped her feet into flat pumps just as the doorbell rang.

* * *

Ruairi was leaning against the doorframe when she opened the door. He was wearing black jeans again but this time with a white polo shirt that showed off his tan skin, the width of his shoulders, the breadth of his chest, and the muscular contours of his upper arms. She stared at him, mesmerized by his tawny good looks and the smile in his hazel eyes. It was a smile that faded as he looked at her and tried to pretend he hadn't noticed her soft curves, the full pout of her lips, and the tentative promise in her eyes.

It was a long time before either of them spoke and when they did they both spoke at the same time. Then they laughed and the tension broke.

"Are you ready for today's mystery tour?" he asked at the same moment that the telephone rang yet again.

Gesturing for him to follow her, she hurried back inside the house to answer it. It was Jenny, again.

"The park at midday," she said. "It's all arranged. All the children will be there. Don't worry about bringing a picnic, we'll have plenty of food."

"I...Jenny what's this all about? I didn't agree to anything. I said I'd call you back after I'd spoken to Ruairi," Maggie protested, hot color flaming her cheeks.

"Well you're too late. We went ahead and organized it without you. As it's such a lovely day the men are all taking the afternoon off work, including Mark. He wants to spend some time with the girls because he says he hasn't seen enough of them lately."

And whose fault is that Maggie wanted to shout into the phone. He could have come home from the hospital every night to put them to bed, and then gone back again later. She didn't say it though. She knew when she was beaten. If Mark was going to the picnic then it was up to her to make sure that Sophie and Amy were too.

"We'll be there," she said, and banged the phone back into the receiver.

"Problems?" Ruairi, still looking just as devastating, was now propped against the kitchen counter.

Briefly she explained the situation to him. He stared at her, started to say something, changed his mind, and then gave a shrug of resignation.

"The park it will have to be then."

"You don't have to come. I can take them in my car if you wouldn't mind giving me a lift home to collect it." She shook her head, trying not to let her frustration show.

"I know I don't have to, but if it means I can spend another day with you then I want to." Without allowing himself think about the implications of what he was about to do, he moved around the end of the kitchen counter so that it was no longer between them, and took her in his arms.

"This is getting ridiculous Maggie! When Sophie and Amy are not demanding your full attention then the rest of the Silver family is outflanking me. What does it take to get some private down time with a girl around here?"

"Depends on the girl," she whispered, raising her face to his.

A sound that was halfway between a sigh and a groan escaped him as he captured her mouth, and for a long moment he was only aware of the questing softness of hcr lips and the sensuous movement of her arms as she slid them up and around his neck. For one blissful moment it was just the two of them. Then it was over.

"Ruairi's here! Ruairi's here!" Sophie burst into the kitchen with a gleeful shout, closely followed by her small sister.

"Hello you two," he released Maggie and caught the little girls to him with an upward swing of his arms. They squealed with excitement and when he put them down, begged for more.

"Not now," he said. "Later, when we're at the park. We're going for a picnic with all your cousins and your aunties and uncles."

"Hurray! Hurray! Hurray." The children started to run around the kitchen in circles, too charged with excited energy to stand still.

"Will Emma be there?" Sophie asked. Emma was her oldest cousin and Sophie's biggest ambition was to be like her.

"Everyone will be there, even Daddy. So hurry up and find your sandals. We'll take your bathing costumes this time too so that you can paddle in the stream without getting your clothes wet." Maggie had recovered her poise even though she could still feel the pressure of Ruairi's hands around her waist and the warmth of his lips on hers. Not allowing herself to think what the kiss might mean, she hurried to collect the things they would need for their trip to the park.

By the time she returned to the kitchen carrying towels and bathing suits Ruairi had lifted both little girls onto the kitchen counter and was fastening their sandals. She smiled her thanks, checked they had both been to the bathroom, and then lifted them down and shooed them towards the front door. Stuffing everything into June's capacious bag, she followed them.

In another minute the door was locked and Ruairi was strapping the children in the car for what seemed like the umpteenth time in the past few days. He straightened up as Maggie opened the trunk and threw the bag in, along with a picnic blanket and cotton jumpers for the girls.

"I mean to do that again just as soon as I can get you alone," he told her.

She smiled up at him, her heart suddenly singing. "I know," she said.

* * *

The picnic in the park was fun. Everybody enjoyed it. The children because they always had a good time when they were together, especially when Auntie Maggie was around to play with them, and it was even better now that Ruairi was there too; all the adults because they felt they were doing the right thing for Mark and June and the children, the sort of thing Cathy Silver would have organized if she hadn't been away on a cruise; and Mark, because being there assuaged the guilt he felt for spending so much time at the hospital with June and the baby when he should have been helping Maggie a bit more with Sophie and Amy.

But most of all, Maggie enjoyed it. Irritated as she was with her family's well-intentioned interference, she now knew that the message she had seen in Ruairi's eyes was real, and it was enough. Soon June would be home, and her mother too, and then she and Ruairi would be able to get to know one another properly without the past getting in the way, because when he had kissed her it had been quite obvious that her childhood was the last thing on his mind. She pushed all thoughts of his departure to Mexico right out of her head. Time enough for that later.

With a shout of laughter she kicked off her shoes and chased her nephews and nieces all over the park while her brothers and sisters-in-law looked on fondly, happy that they were helping out.

Ruairi watched too, from behind his sunglasses. Officially he was sitting with the men, talking about male things, and to all outward appearances he was indeed having a deep conversation about the latest cricket scores and the likely future success of the English cricket team. It was only taking a fraction of his attention though. The rest of it was on Maggie as she splashed in the shallow stream with Sophie and Amy, holding tightly to their hands to make sure they didn't slip. Then he watched her help them to collect twigs and feathers and some of the leathery leaves which were already beginning to fall from the trees thanks to a prolonged hot spell. He saw her fashion them into a boat and then she was lost in the melee as the rest of the children joined her, demanding she show them how to do it too.

"I think Maggie could do with a bit of help," he said, pushing himself up from the grass and walking casually across to where she sat on the bank of the shallow stream.

"Don't you believe it," Peter called after him. "She loves it all as much as the children."

Ruairi ignored him as he sat down beside her. "Hello you," he said.

She smiled at him. "You've escaped then?"

"Mmm. Ouch! I didn't see that coming," he gasped for breath as Amy jumped on him, and after that the rest of the afternoon was spent refereeing boat races.

It doesn't matter though, thought Maggie, glancing across to where Ruairi was concentrating on a minor repair. Soon we'll go home and the children will go to bed, and Mark will go to the hospital to see June, and then we'll be able to talk. She wouldn't let herself think about what else they might do. What it would actually be like to kiss Ruairi again without any fear of interruption.

And when he turned towards her and saw her looking at him she knew, from his smile, that he was thinking exactly the same thing, and she felt her heart begin to turn slow somersaults in her chest.

It wasn't to be though, for as soon as everyone began to make a move to leave, Mark came across to where she and Ruairi were sitting.

"If you'll give me the keys to your car I'll move the children's car seats back into mine and take everyone home," he told Ruairi. "I'm not going to see June tonight. I popped in before I came to the park and she said she wants to rest so she won't be too tired when I take Sophie and Amy in to see her tomorrow."

He turned to Maggie then. "She said to tell you she'd love to see you tomorrow too if you can manage it. Once Sophie and Amy have seen the baby, it's open house, so I've said I'll babysit while you visit her in the evening."

"Of course I'd love to see her and the baby," she said. "Everyone would. We've just been waiting for the all clear."

"I know! And she feels bad about having kept everyone away but she's just been too worried to cope with having visitors until now."

"It's okay Mark. Everyone understands." Maggie touched his arm sympathetically, Ruairi forgotten for a moment when she saw the strained expression shadowing her brother's eyes and realized he was still traumatized by the events of the past few days.

Ruairi, however, had not forgotten Maggie. If he had thought he was frustrated before, when he was trying to keep his distance, it was nothing to how he felt now he'd declared his feelings. Well, started to declare them if the truth be told, because there was no time to finish anything in the busy chaos that was the Silver family. And unless he got some time alone with her soon he would never be able to sort out the muddle of his emotions, or find out how serious she was about him. It was obvious from the strain on Mark's face, however, that he still needed her support, so he searched around for a possible solution.

"Why don't I collect a takeaway for the three of us for later?" he said.

"Thanks but I'd rather pass tonight if you don't mind," Mark shook his head as he collected his small daughters and began to herd them towards his car. "I've been living on fast food for days at the hospital so I'm looking forward to some of Maggie's home cooking. Besides, I need to catch up with work. There are a lot of emails that I must answer before I start my paternity leave."

* * *

While Mark sorted out Sophie and Amy, Maggie and Ruairi walked back to where the others were clearing up so Maggie could retrieve her belongings. Although there was a sizeable space between them they could both feel the tingle of attraction. It's almost as if we're magnetized, Maggie thought. If I took one step towards him I'm sure we'd fuse together. The thought made her stomach flip. So did Mark's plans, but in a bad way.

"I'm sorry," she said, her voice low.

"So am I!" The expression on Ruairi's face was unexpectedly grim.

"Will I…will we see you tomorrow?" she asked, suddenly less sure of herself. Had her family wrecked a relationship between her and Ruairi before it even started? Was he so fed up with being hijacked that he was just going to walk away?

"Tomorrow you're going to see Jo," he reminded her. "And then in the evening you're going to see June and the baby."

"The day after then?" Any pride she might have had, had gone.

He looked at her and she could see he was struggling to suppress his irritation. "Maybe, but no plans. Not even a time. Instead I'll call you first thing in the morning. That way we might avoid tempting fate, or at least giving your family a chance to disrupt our agenda."

She nodded, too disappointed to smile, and the last thing Ruairi saw before he turned away was her bottom lip trembling.

Chapter Eleven

It was a long evening for Ruairi. His mother was still visiting friends and would not return to the hotel until the following afternoon; there was nothing that he wanted to watch on the huge, flat screen television that dominated the hotel suite; he couldn't concentrate on reading; and he wasn't feeling sociable enough to call anyone. So, with the aim of keeping his mind away from Maggie for at least an hour or two, he decided to tackle his own backlog of work and dug his laptop out of his half unpacked luggage.

Two hours later he was still busy when a new email pinged onto the screen. Recognizing the sender he opened it immediately, read it, re-read it, and then read it a third time. As soon as he'd answered it he sat back and stared at the blank television screen on the other side of the room. He needed to do something. If he'd had company he'd have suggested a celebratory drink. As it was he called the only person who he could think of who would appreciate how he was feeling. He called Jo.

"Hello," she sounded sleepy.

Belatedly he remembered the jetlag. "Sorry! Did I wake you?"

She laughed. "Not a chance! I've slept so much today that I'm likely to be up all night."

"You're okay then?"

"I'm absolutely fine and I'm looking forward to seeing Maggie again tomorrow. You didn't tell me what a sweetheart she is."

"I guess I didn't." His reply was deliberately dismissive. He would have to face up to whatever Maggie was beginning to mean to him soon enough now that he'd shown his hand, and when that happened he didn't want advice or encouragement from anyone, not even Jo. The time he'd spent with the Silver family had already persuaded him that both could be the kiss of death in some situations.

"Well, what do you want?" Jo was waiting. She had known him a long time. Ruairi never called to pass the time of day and although his dismissive remark hadn't fooled her one little bit, she knew that if he didn't want to discuss Maggie then they wouldn't be discussing Maggie.

He took a deep breath, hardly able to believe what he was going to tell her. "I've just received an email from Blake Wallis Productions."

He removed the phone from his ear as her squeal of excitement nearly burst his eardrum. When he started listening again she was full of questions.

"They've bought it then, your documentary idea, with you presenting? When will it be shown? Where will it be shown?"

"Hang on! It's not quite so cut and dried as that. You know how it works Jo. Blake Wallis

139

has expressed an interest and someone from the company wants to talk to me about my idea as soon as possible. I guess I just take it from there."

"When do they want to see you?"

"As soon as I can manage it," his voice dipped a bit as he told her that.

She heard it. "Is that a problem? I know you're on holiday but surely this is too important."

"Of course it is. I've already told them I'll be there on Tuesday."

"And…?"

"And nothing."

"Hmm. You wouldn't want me to explain to Maggie about how important this is for your career would you?"

He sighed. Was he really that transparent?

Before he decided how to reply Jo started talking again. "Don't answer that. Just do me a favor in return. I know you'll be talking to Ollie about this so, when you do, would you remind him he needs to be over here in four weeks time latest unless he wants to risk his son being born without him."

"Will do." Glad to have escaped further questioning, Ruairi talked about Ollie and their forthcoming baby for a few more minutes and then, accepting her congratulations for a second time, finished the call.

Abandoning his computer he walked across the room to the minibar, poured a generous measure of whisky into a cut glass tumbler, and took it out onto the balcony. Directly above him a scatter of pale stars were strewn across the night sky. Below him the reflection of the pilot lights on the moored boats twinkled on the water. Further off he could hear the drone of traffic and see the faint orange glow where the street lamps faded out the stars altogether.

As he sipped his whisky he was suddenly seized with a fierce longing for the clear southern sky that had been so much a part of his life when he was working in New Zealand. He would love to show it to Maggie. He knew just how she would look as she gazed up at it and saw the huge nebula of the Milky Way surrounded by the glitter of millions and trillions of stars. In his mind's eye he could see her lying back on the sand and staring up at a sky untroubled by the sodium glare of street lamps, a sky that looked as it might have looked when earth was dawning. And he would lie back on the sand with her and when she had finished looking they would…abruptly he drained his glass and went back inside. It wouldn't do to think about it, not now he'd heard from Blake Wallis Productions, because if his meeting with them was successful then it was going to turn his life upside down for weeks into the future. There would be no down time, no time for Maggie at all.

Closing his email server he clicked on a file on his computer and opened it. A picture of a tiny blue penguin flashed on the screen. Without being able to help himself, he smiled. Henriqué!

He'd given him his name the first time he saw him, unable to help himself because although all the penguins were amusing, Henriqué was the funniest of all with his exaggeratedly slouchy shoulders and a braying call that was so loud compared to the rest of the penguins that it sounded like a donkey in pain.

After looking at the image for a moment longer he scrolled down and started to read the accompanying text. It was full of details about the colony where Henriqué lived. It described the life cycle of the three hundred penguins, their breeding season, the days they spent at sea. He'd spent weeks researching everything about them and then he'd added the comic slant that he'd hoped would be the thing to fire the imagination of an editor looking for a new idea.

He finished forty minutes later, closed the file and the computer, and poured himself a second glass of whisky. Sipping it reflectively, he allowed himself a brief moment of congratulation. His idea worked. It really worked. He'd found the little penguins so amusing every time he'd watched them that he'd eventually taken a chance with it and sent his idea to a film production company that specialized in wild life documentaries, hoping that what he was offering was just different enough to intrigue. Then he'd tried to forget about it because he knew it would be a while before he received a response. Now that someone in the company had expressed an interest he knew hoops would have to be jumped. There were no guarantees but at least he was halfway there.

Hopefully he had found exactly the thing to move him on in his career. For a long time he'd been toying with the idea of making and presenting his own documentaries instead of just filming them for other people, and now it looked as if he was about the get the chance. It was the opportunity he had been striving for, or it had been until he met Maggie again and she had driven everything from his mind except the need to be with her whatever it took. She had taken over his thoughts to such an extent that when the email had arrived on his screen it had been like a message from a former life. His life before Maggie!

Now the two had converged, however, he was going to have to do something about it. He frowned, abandoned his half empty glass on the coffee table, and made his way out to the balcony again. How could he make it fit?

Since this morning when, unable to help himself any longer, he had at last lowered his defenses and kissed Maggie, he was in no doubt that she felt the same about him. Would it be enough though? She was so passionate about her own plans, so determined to take her teaching skills to where she thought they were needed, that it wouldn't be fair to ask her to give them up. He couldn't do it and live with himself, particularly when he knew that after a few months she would begin to resent the weeks he would have to spend away from her while he concentrated on his own career. Time away from family was something that was part and parcel of the life he had chosen and if Blake Wallis was truly interested in his documentary idea then it would quickly get a lot worse. He wouldn't have a minute to call his own if he had to start travelling between England and New Zealand on a regular basis while also trying to fit in the work he had agreed to do in Mexico.

He had to face it. His first thoughts about starting a relationship with Maggie had been the right ones after all. Working as he did didn't fit with family life and he was not prepared to insult her by offering anything less. Maggie was forever or she wasn't at all.

* * *

Maggie was clearing up the kitchen when Ruairi's email arrived, and by the time he had finished his call to Jo she had moved on to the pile of ironing waiting in the laundry basket. That finished, she popped her head into the study where Mark was working and asked him if he needed anything.

He shook his head, too busy at his computer screen to do more than mumble his thanks.

"I'm off to bed then," she told him. "And you should go too Mark. You need to sleep while you can. As soon as the baby comes home you'll have disturbed nights for weeks."

144

He shrugged impatiently. "It doesn't work like that sis. Work won't go away just because we have a new baby. You'll see, eventually!"

She didn't bother to answer. Nor did she slam the door behind her, although she wanted to, and it wasn't because she didn't want to upset Mark, it was because she didn't want to wake Sophie and Amy.

Did he think she was a complete idiot? Of course she knew life went on, new baby or not. But she also knew he was going to knock himself out from lack of sleep if he wasn't careful and then what use would he be to June and the children. She just had to hope that her mother would make him see sense when she arrived home. In the meantime she was going to stop trying. It was enough that she was spending every minute of every day looking after his children and his house so he could be with June.

She thought about her sister-in-law and wondered how she was feeling, all alone in the hospital, worrying about her baby. She hoped that June's parents might come over this time. They had visited when Sophie was born but they hadn't been able to manage another trip two years later for Amy, and there had never been any question of June and Mark being able to afford a trip to Australia to see them with the girls. Poor June must be so lonely. It must be the same for Jo too.

She stopped cleaning off her make-up and stared at herself in the mirror. Why hadn't she thought of it before? She would introduce them to one another. They had such a lot in common what with busy husbands, new babies and families far away. Besides Jo had told her she'd spent quite a lot of time in Australia before she moved on to New Zealand, so surely that would help them gel too. She would talk to Jo about it tomorrow, and then to June in the evening when she visited her to see her new nephew.

Satisfied she had made a good decision she finished getting ready for bed and then settled herself against her pillows and opened the book she had been reading on and off for the past week. After five minutes she threw it down. She must have read the same page at least four times and she still didn't know what it said. All she did know was that while the words danced up and down in front of her eyes, her brain insisted on thinking about Ruairi.

She sighed. He had been so fed up when she left the park with Mark and the children and yet what had she been supposed to do? Mark was relying on her to feed him and Sophie and Amy and then put the girls to bed while he tackled his backlog of work. Nor could she let June down. For a moment she felt irritated with Ruairi. Why couldn't he see what a difficult situation she was in?

Then she remembered how patient he'd been, how he had looked after her and the children and fitted his days around their needs, and she felt ashamed she could be so ungrateful. She remembered, too, how he'd been there for her when June and the baby had been in such

146

danger, and how he'd held her close. And now it had happened again and for just one moment this morning, when she was in his arms and his mouth was on hers, she had really believed he felt the same as she did. Then Sophie and Amy had charged into the room and disturbed them and they had never had a moment alone together again. She squeezed her eyes tight shut against the tears that were threatening, and refused to think about what had happened between them because she knew it wasn't going to happen again, not after obvious irritation and his casual farewell at the park.

Not that she could blame him for not making a definite arrangement to meet up again. It would take the patience of a saint to put up with her family. She wondered what he was doing now. Probably meeting up with real friends, like Jo. People who shared his world instead of those who had closed the gap he had left behind when he started travelling.

She thought about his words, about how her own travel plans might make her susceptible to the same isolation when she returned; how situations and people would move on while she was away; and she wondered if it would upset her or whether she would just accept it as the price she had to pay for the freedom to make her own life.

With a sob of frustration she punched her pillow into a more comfortable shape, turned on her side and switched off the bedside light. She would go to sleep and forget about Ruairi because she needed all the sleep she could get before Sophie and Amy invaded her bed on the dot of six-thirty in the morning. He would either call her the day after tomorrow or he wouldn't, and if he didn't then she couldn't really blame him.

Her plan didn't work though. She was still awake when Mark finally finished his work and climbed the stairs to go to bed, and she was still awake an hour later when Amy woke up from a bad dream. By the time she had soothed her back to sleep, dawn was already streaking the sky and she watched the clouds turn from grey to pink to orange as she waited for the day to begin.

* * *

The children kept Maggie very busy the following morning. They were so full of excitement at the prospect of going to the hospital to visit their new brother that they squabbled about absolutely everything. In desperation she found paper, glue and coloring pencils and helped them make cards for him and for June. Then, because there was still time to spare before lunch, she showed them how to cut out chains of paper dolls. Finally quiet, they concentrated on drawing faces and dresses on the dolls while she rustled up a simple lunch of scrambled eggs and beans.

By the time Mark returned from work to collect them, she had dressed them in their prettiest dresses, made sure they had clean hands and faces and that their hair was brushed, and had also found envelopes for the cards they had made. She watched as they followed him to his car and climbed inside. They waved excitedly as he pulled away. Maggie waved too and then she returned to the house with a sigh of relief and closed the door behind her.

It only took a few minutes to clear up the lunch dishes, then she was free for the whole afternoon. She smiled at her reflection in the mirror as she tidied her hair. She was looking forward to seeing Jo again. She wanted to learn more about her life and what it was that had made her brave enough to set out into the world alone. She wanted to find out more about Ruairi too. Jo knew him as he was now, her memories were not confused with the boy he used to be, and she needed that. She wanted to know everything there was to know about the real Ruairi. With that in mind she pulled the front door shut behind her, ignoring a sudden sinking feeling in the pit of her stomach that told her that if he didn't telephone her tomorrow, then anything she learned about him from Jo would just be dust in the wind.

* * *

"Maggie! Come in! I'm so glad to see you," Jo's welcome was warm as she led her into the apartment.

Maggie looked around with astonishment. Jo had only been in the country for forty-eight hours and yet she had already managed to turn the soulless apartment into a home. A brightly colored cotton blanket was draped across the back of the sofa, there were photos on the windowsill, candles and a scatter of small items on every other surface, and a pile of paperbacks on the coffee table. She could smell coffee brewing too, and biscuits had already been piled onto a plate.

"This looks so welcoming," she exclaimed. "I thought it would take days for you to settle in."

Jo laughed. "In my job, home is wherever I put my rucksack down, so I've gotten used to carrying around the things that keep it familiar."

"It's lovely. Oh, is this you and Ollie on your wedding day." Maggie had wandered across to the window and she picked up a photo frame while Jo poured coffee.

Putting the full mugs onto the coffee table, Jo took it from her with a smile. "Yes. It's the only photo I have that proves he owns a suit and a tie!"

"Have many of your colleagues started relationships at work," Maggie was eager to learn more about the life that was so much a part of Ruairi, although she hoped Jo wouldn't think she was being too curious.

"Mmm quite a few actually. I think we end up together because of the amount of time we spend in each other's company when we're away on long trips. I often tell Ollie that if it wasn't for my job I wouldn't have given him so much as a second look!"

Maggie laughed at her jokey words even though they pierced her heart. How stupid of her to even think she might be in Ruairi's league. She was far too naïve to interest someone like him for long. Despite his patience and kindness and the fact that he obviously found her attractive, Jo's casual remark confirmed what she already feared, that he was just killing time with her while his mother enjoyed her holiday.

She should have realized he was at a lose end when he told her he had already distanced himself from most of his old friends by spending too many years abroad. He was probably counting the days to when he could leave the Silver family and domesticity behind him and get back to the people who shared his world. Maybe there was already someone in that world who was waiting for him to come back to her; someone far more interesting and experienced than a red-headed primary school teacher whose idea of travel to date was a two-week family holiday in Europe. As the truth hit her, the crack that had started to zigzag across her heart suddenly split right open so that for a moment she could barely breathe.

By the time she started listening again Jo was talking about other things and she forced herself to ask the right questions about the baby and about her and Ollie's plans for the future.

"We've taken this apartment for three months," Jo explained. "After that, all being well, we'll be on the move again. We'll spend a few more months in New Zealand and then it will probably be South America although that will depend on whether we can get joint contracts."

"You mean, you'll be taking the baby with you?"

"Well we certainly don't intend to leave him behind," Jo chuckled as she refilled Maggie's coffee mug and pushed the plate of biscuits towards her.

"But won't it be difficult…I mean what will happen if he gets sick?"

"Then I expect I'll worry just like all every other parent," Jo gave a slight frown. Then she smiled. "The thing is Maggie, work doesn't go away when babies arrive. Ollie and I were in the middle of a big project when I discovered I was pregnant, and if we want to get paid then we have to finish it. I had to come home while I was still allowed to fly but it's why Ollie is still in New Zealand, and it's also why he won't be joining me here until closer to the time the baby is due. Besides, children are very adaptable. I know from personal experience because both my parents are archeologists so I rarely spent longer than a couple of years in any one place when I was small."

Hearing Jo echo the words about work and babies that Mark had thrown at her the previous evening, Maggie suddenly felt very confused.

Brought up in a family where everyone tried to manage everyone else, and where there was always a grandparent or an aunt or an uncle to take over in an emergency, she had never really thought about what happened in other families. Jo's matter-of-fact attitude gave her pause for thought as she suddenly realized it was entirely possible to live a very different sort of life perfectly successfully. The model of family life she had been brought up with was not the only one, so her plan to travel and work abroad for a few years before returning home to settle down wasn't necessarily her only choice.

"Your life is so different from mine," she told Jo shyly. "I can't imagine living like that. How will you cope with six months in suburbia?"

"Very well indeed." Jo smiled at her. "Just because I spend most of my life camping in the middle of nowhere doesn't mean I don't enjoy the fleshpots of civilized life when I get the chance."

"I don't think you'll find many fleshpots around here," Maggie said with a laugh, and after that they talked about other things, including June and the baby. Jo was very enthusiastic about the thought of meeting her and she wanted to see Sophie and Amy again too.

Despite her original plan, it wasn't until Maggie was getting ready to leave that they talked about Ruairi.

"Isn't it great news about Ruairi's documentary?" Jo called out as she carried the empty coffee mugs through to the kitchen. "He phoned me last night to tell me about it. He was so thrilled. He deserves it too. He's worked so hard for this."

Maggie, following her with the remains of the biscuits, almost dropped the pretty china plate she was carrying when she learned Ruairi had phoned Jo with some exciting news. Although she was glad for him she couldn't shake off a feeling of jealousy. She wanted to be the one he talked to when something happened that was important to his career and yet, far from sharing things with her, he had even refused to make any arrangements for the following day. The misery she had been keeping at bay while she talked to Jo deepened. What if he really did fail to phone her tomorrow despite his half promise? How would she deal with it when she could feel jealous over such a trivial thing as this? Not wanting Jo to know how she felt, nor that she didn't know a thing about Ruairi's exciting news, she forced out an ambiguous reply.

"It sounds wonderful."

"Yes it does, although I guess it will cut his holiday a bit short because the Production Company is sure to want him to go back to New Zealand as soon as possible so he can get things moving."

She looked at Maggie then, having finished sliding the uneaten biscuits into a plastic box.

Maggie met her blue gaze with level eyes and kept her voice steady as she replied.

"Well I hope he doesn't plan on going before his mother has finished her holiday because I don't think she likes travelling on her own."

* * *

Later, when she visited the hospital, she kept her mind focused on her sister-in-law and her new nephew.

"He's absolutely gorgeous," she told June. "And you too. I thought you would be looking tired and ill but you look wonderful."

"That's all the hormones surging through me, I expect," June replied with a smile as she lifted her tiny son from his cot and handed him to Maggie.

Cuddling him, Maggie asked if they had chosen a name for him yet.

June grinned at her. "Yes. We talked to Sophie and Amy about it today. It took us a while to persuade them that Mickey, Donald or Pluto weren't really what we were looking for and eventually they agreed to settle for John."

Knowing how pleased her Dad would be that they were naming the baby after him, Maggie squeezed her sister-in-law's hand. Then she told her about Jo and how much she was looking forward to introducing them to one another. Just before she left, June thanked her, yet again, for looking after Mark and the children.

"And I believe I have to thank Ruairi and his mother too," she said. "Sophie and Amy hardly stopped talking about him and Mrs. O'Connor the whole time they were here."

"Yes. Ruairi and his mum have been marvelous," Maggie agreed. "I'm not sure how we would have coped without them."

Chapter Twelve

Both Maggie and Ruairi spent a lot of time looking at the phone the following morning; Ruairi because he wasn't sure what he was going to say; Maggie because she was willing it to ring.

When it finally did ring, however, she was outside pegging out wet towels, so Sophie answered it. Maggie could hear her excitement from halfway down the garden. She hurried back to the kitchen and found her small niece perched on a kitchen stool with her legs crossed, looking like somebody's miniature Personal Assistant.

"That will be fine," she was saying in a voice that was a fair imitation of her mother's. "I'll tell Auntie Maggie to be ready by one o'clock."

Then, before Maggie could seize the handset or Ruairi had time to ask to speak to her, she cut the call and returned the phone to its receiver.

"Ruairi is taking us to the cinema," she announced. "He's collecting us at one o' clock."

"How kind of him." Maggie, who knew that a newly released Disney film was on at the local cinema, forced a smile, even though she was irritated he hadn't thought to check that the arrangements fitted with her own plans.

And how clever of him too, she thought, as she returned to the garden to finish pegging out the laundry. We won't be able to talk in the cinema with the two children sitting between us and then, after that, they will be so full of chatter while he drives us home, that we might well manage to say goodbye without a single word of any real importance passing between us.

She was preparing an early lunch when the phone rang again.

"I'm…um…I'm just calling to check that the cinema trip is okay with you. Sophie rang off in such a hurry that we didn't have a chance to speak." Ruairi's voice at the other end of the line was more tentative than usual and the note of underlying laughter was missing.

"It's fine. In fact it's very kind of you. The children are really excited. They have been asking Mark to take them for days."

"You're okay with it then," she could hear the relief in his voice. "It just felt a bit high handed to arrange everything with Sophie without her giving me a chance to talk to you."

Despite everything, Maggie's laughter was genuine. "You don't need to worry about that. Sophie is not my mother's granddaughter for nothing. She's a natural organizer so if Sophie says we're going to the cinema, then we're going to the cinema!"

She didn't receive the expected chuckle in return, however. Instead Ruairi just confirmed he would pick them up at one and rang off, convincing Maggie even more that he was getting bored with the whole Silver family scenario that had unwittingly enfolded him, and that he couldn't wait to return to his work and to the peace of New Zealand.

* * *

As she had anticipated, Maggie didn't have a chance to say anything personal to Ruairi in the car, nor as they made their way to the cinema with the excited children skipping and hopping beside them. Instead she had to wait until they were ensconced in their seats, with Sophie and Amy between them, before she could congratulate him on his documentary.

"You've been talking to Jo," he gave a wry smile as their eyes met over the top of the children's heads.

She nodded, determined to seem enthusiastic. After all the interest he'd shown in her own half-formed travel plans, and the time he had devoted to her and the children even though it had probably bored him half to death, the least she could do was convince him she was really pleased about his news.

"It's not a foregone conclusion yet whatever Jo told you. I've a meeting with someone at the production company on Tuesday. Until then I can't be sure of anything."

"But assuming the company does give you the go ahead, what happens next?" Maggie's voice was cheerful and her expression full of interest as she pursued the details of what she knew would only be bad news as far as she was concerned.

"I'm not sure but it will almost certainly mean I have to go back to New Zealand for a while before I start my next job…" Ruairi's voice tailed off as the lights in the auditorium faded and Sophie silenced him with a fierce whisper.

"Sorry!" he whispered back. Then he settled into his seat, ready to watch the film.

* * *

Maggie looked up at the huge screen without seeing anything at all. All she could focus on were Ruairi's last words. Tuesday and then New Zealand! If all went as he hoped it would, then in two days time he would be gone from her life and she would have to find a way to fill the blank days and weeks he would leave behind. She clenched her hands so tightly her nails dug into her palms. It stopped the tears though. She wished she could find something as simple to stop the ache in her heart.

Ruairi, after the first five minutes, gave up looking at the screen at all. Instead he watched Maggie and saw how the light and color flickering from the screen shadowed her high cheekbones and made her eyes glitter and her hair spark with red fire. Then, as the scenes on the screen in front of them changed, she would be briefly plunged into darkness. Barely able to see the outline of the soft curve of her mouth and her small straight nose, he would wait for it to start all over again, and with every new illumination his heart twisted and turned like a mad thing. How could he bear to say goodbye? How could he just walk away when he wanted her so much?

For long moments, as the animated characters on the screen laughed and sang, and as they completed impossible tasks and won impossible races, he tussled with his dilemma. What if he told Maggie how he felt about her and then spelt out exactly what a life with him would entail, would that solve everything? If he explained about the long absences and how he often had to live for weeks on end in isolated places, and she decided that, despite everything, she wanted him, then his problem was solved.

Then he thought about what his life was really like; the months away from home, the long, long weeks out in the field, the hours spent editing film, the extra work his own documentary would entail, and he knew he couldn't do it to her. She needed more than that. She needed to live her own life, not spend her time waiting for him. He was just going to have to be tough for both of them because however much she might think she wanted him right now, it wouldn't last. He had seen how the long weeks apart had caused too many of his

161

colleagues' marriages to fail to feel confident enough to take the plunge. He did owe her an explanation though after what he'd said to her the day they went to the park.

* * *

The journey home was full of noise and laughter as Sophie and Amy, with Maggie's help, sang some of the songs from the film, and then pretended to be the main characters, speaking to one another in squeaky voices and then dissolving into fits of laughter until they became thoroughly over-excited. In the end Maggie calmed them down by telling them a story. Listening to the soft cadences of her voice Ruairi felt curiously soothed and relaxed by the time he pulled into the curb outside Mark's house.

"I enjoyed that," he told her as the girls leapt from the car and rushed up the path to find their father so they could tell him about the film.

She smiled at him as she shook her head. "Fairy stories Mr. O'Connor! I'm sure you should have progressed further than that by now!"

He chuckled. "Maybe I prefer to stay in first grade because of the teacher."

Their eyes met as he spoke and although she smiled at his teasing, Maggie's face reflected the hurt of so many unanswered questions that he suddenly found it hard to draw breath into his lungs. Had he done that to her? If he had then he needed to put it right. Before he had a chance to utter a word, however, Mark called to them both from the front door.

"Come on you two. I've put some beers in the fridge and a bottle of wine too."

Without a word they both turned towards the house, Ruairi flicking the automatic car lock with his finger as he followed Maggie. Seeing the proud tilt of her head and the straight lines of her slim back he knew she would be devastated to know that he had seen right through her, had seen in her eyes the exact same expression she had worn when he'd first left to start his travels all those years ago, and, just like then, he didn't know what to do about it.

* * *

"Here, catch!" Mark tossed a can of beer at him as he walked into the kitchen. "How about we sit in the garden while Maggie feeds the kids and gets them ready for bed? Then I'll get a take-away meal for the three of us."

When Ruairi didn't immediately answer, he added, "I'm sorry about the other night. I just had too much to do, but I've caught up now. I'm not going to the hospital this evening either as so many other people are visiting. Besides, the doc has said June and the baby can come home tomorrow, so this will probably be our last chance to have a drink together for quite a while."

163

When she heard his news Maggie stopped smarting over being relegated to the kitchen to give the girls their tea while Mark and Ruairi drank beer, and gave her brother a hug.

"That's marvelous news. Did you hear what Daddy said girls? Mummy will be bringing your new brother home very soon."

Immediately both children were full of plans and they ate everything she put before them, too busy discussing the special cake they were going to make for their brother, and what colour balloons they were going to put up to welcome him home, to remember to be picky about their tea.

Pleased for June, who she knew was anxious to come home, Maggie joined in enthusiastically, and by the time they were ready for bed a full campaign had been launched. It included baking, going shopping to buy presents, and making sure that the house was tidy. With pink faces and damp hair the children rushed downstairs in their pajamas to relay their plans to Mark. As soon as she had emptied the bath, hung up the wet towels and tossed the children's dirty clothes into the laundry basket, Maggie followed.

She found them sitting on Mark's lap while he listened and nodded and tried to look suitably impressed in all the right places. Ruairi, sprawled in a chair opposite, was smiling, and it was a smile that widened when he saw Maggie.

"Come and sit down. I'll open the wine unless you'd prefer beer."

"No…a glass of wine would be lovely…but I'll have it later, once I've put the girls to bed."

"I'm sure Mark can do that," Ruairi's voice was unexpectedly firm. "You've been looking after them all day so it's time you had a break."

His remark took Mark by surprise and for just a moment he looked irritated but then, astonishingly, he gave Maggie an apologetic smile. "Sorry sis. I should have thought. Of course I'll put them to bed. Come on you two. Kiss Auntie Maggie and Ruairi goodnight and then you can finish telling me what's going to happen tomorrow while you get into bed."

Still excited, the children's kisses were perfunctory as they rushed from the room, but as they climbed the stairs, Maggie and Ruairi could still hear them. "And we're going to ask Ruairi to help us blow up the balloons 'cos he's got the biggest puff," Sophie told her father, while Amy explained that Granny 'Connor was going to help bake the cake.

"Cos she likes making cakes," she explained. "'Cept she doesn't have any little girls and boys to make them for now, not since Auntie Maggie and Ruairi got all growed up."

Maggie and Ruairi looked at one another. Then Ruairi laughed.

"I guess Mum and I are back here again tomorrow then, if you'll have us. And the two of them are spot on about me… having the biggest puff I mean."

"And about your Mum having nobody to bake cakes for, too," Maggie added quietly.

The laughter faded from his face, leaving him looking sad as well as much older than he had a moment before because her words had reminded him of the other dilemma in his life. "That too!"

"It must be very difficult for you now she's alone," she said, her own woes temporarily forgotten as her warm heart remembered that Mrs. O'Connor would soon be on her own again, in Ireland, far away from her old friends and far away from Ruairi as well.

He nodded. "I haven't done a very good job of looking after her so far either. I thought regular phone calls were enough until I arrived back in Ireland and saw how much she had aged since Dad died. She never complains you see. She always says everything is fine when I call, and until I saw her, I believed her."

"But as soon as you realized, you arranged this holiday for her and she's loving every minute of it," Maggie reminded him. Although her own heart was breaking at the thought that he'd soon be gone from her own life, she still wanted to wipe away the bleak expression on his face and the furrow that had appeared between his eyes.

He shook his head. "A holiday is easy Maggie. It's the rest of the year that's the problem. She really needs to move back here, to where all her old friends are. It's what she wants to do too, but I'm not sure how she'll manage it on her own. I won't be able to help her either. Not for a while anyway, and probably not for months if the production company takes out an option on my documentary."

He sighed. "I feel so guilty. She was always a fantastic Mum. You know that. And yet here I am planning to leave her yet again, and for a long time too, when what she really wants is family around her, and grandchildren. Not that she has ever said a word about the life I lead, or even hinted that she thinks I should settle down."

"That's because she's so proud of you," Maggie told him, remembering how Mrs. O'Connor had waxed lyrical about all of Ruairi's many achievements when they'd had lunch together.

It had also been the day when she had put Maggie on high alert to find out what was worrying him as well. Well now she knew exactly what it was. It was Mrs. O'Connor herself. Not Jo, as she had at first so stupidly believed. No! He was worried about how he was going to be able to look after his mother from the other side of the world because he knew there was nobody else to do it.

"Why don't I help her," she blurted out before she could stop herself. "I could go and stay with her during a school vacation and help her to organize everything. Then I could go and fetch her whenever she was ready to move."

Already half out of the armchair, preparing to go into the kitchen to pour her some wine, Ruairi sank back into his seat and stared at her. "Why would you do that?"

"Because we get on really well, and because she was always so good to me when I was small. Helping her to move would be a way to repay her for all her kindness."

"And what about your own travel plans?"

"Oh those! I've sort of put those on hold recently, what with the problems with June and the baby. Besides, even if I do get a teaching contract in another country, I'll still have to give a half term's notice to my school before I can leave, so it will be ages before I can go anywhere."

Maggie had to grace to blush as she stretched the truth. She didn't want him to know that despite her apparent display of enthusiasm when they'd had lunch together, she had not only shelved her travel plans but had actually stacked them in the most inaccessible and dusty compartment of her mind ever since he had come back into her life.

He shook his head and left the room without another word, leaving Maggie to stare out of the window and wonder whether she was simply being altruistic or whether offering to help Mrs. O'Connor was actually her way of making sure she stayed in touch with Ruairi.

When he reappeared with a full glass of wine and she saw him standing in the doorway, the evening sun burnishing his hair, his clear hazel eyes half-closed against the glare, her heart felt as if it was going to thump right through her ribcage. With a feeling of shame she acknowledged the truth. Much as she liked and admired Mrs. O'Connor, and would happily do anything to help her, the real reason for her offer was because it was a way of keeping a part of Ruairi in her life. She took the wine from him with what she hoped was an enthusiastic smile.

"I meant what I said."

"I'm sure you did," his voice was warm and full of gratitude even while he shook his head. "But I can't let you do it Maggie, and nor would Mum. You have too much living of your own to do, too many plans."

"But I told you, even if I find a job tomorrow it will still be months before I can get away."

He took her free hand in his and although the touch of his fingers sent her heart racing, she still heard the finality in his reply. "That's not a good enough reason. You need to get on with your own life and stop letting other people get in the way. Your family already runs you ragged. They take it for granted you'll help out whenever they need you without a thought about what you want for yourself, and as if that isn't enough, now you're thinking of adding someone else to your list."

."I…they're not that bad," her protest was half-hearted as she remembered how she had poured her heart out to him about that very thing when he first came back into her life.

"Yes they are. I know they don't mean to be but if you want an honest opinion then you need to realize that I'd do the same in their situation. If I knew someone who was willing, capable, and good with children, and who was always available to help out, then I'd make sure I took advantage of her. And now you're proposing to add to your burden by taking on an elderly woman who lives in the middle of nowhere in rural Ireland. It makes no sense. Stop finding excuses to dream dreams while doing nothing about them."

"That's not fair!" Two spots of angry color highlighted Maggie's cheeks as she felt the sting of his remark.

"Maybe not, but it's what it looks like from here. Get out and live before it's too late. You've escaped one boyfriend who was perfect husband material if I remember rightly, but if you go on like this you might not have the strength to escape another one."

They stared at one another. Maggie's face was full of hurt pride as she heard the rejection in his voice. Coming so soon after he'd kissed her made it doubly hard to bear. Ruairi, for his part, refused to think about what he was doing to her so sure was he that it was for her own good. He had to cut the ties that were beginning to bind them together before he ruined her life however lonely it made him feel. In the silence that followed his words they heard Mark's feet clattering on the stairs. He released her hand.

"I'm sorry! I had no right. You get enough advice from everyone else," he whispered the moment before Mark came into the room waving the take-away menu and asking for orders.

Chapter Thirteen

The rest of the evening passed Maggie by. Although she dutifully ordered from the take-away menu Mark had found pinned to the kitchen notice board, and although she laid the table while the men went off to collect the food, and although she sat and chatted until it was time for Ruairi to go and fetch his mother from yet another set of friends, she had no recollection of anything that had been said.

As she cleared away the various foil dishes and plastic boxes, and washed up the plates, all she could think about were Ruairi's words. They went round and round in her head until she thought she might scream, not because she was angry with him, but because she knew he was right. Although she had talked a lot about how she was going to change her job and travel the world, it had remained just that. Talk! She hadn't done a single thing about it during the long summer vacation, and she could no longer convince herself that it was because Ruairi had come back into her life because, deep down, she knew it wasn't true. Not really. If she'd really been as serious about travelling as she claimed, then she would have had a definite plan in mind by now. She would have had a job lined up long before her parent's ruby wedding.

Standing in front of the kitchen sink, her hands elbow deep in soapy water, she stared out of the window into the garden. Although it was dark, the solar powered lamps Mark had installed the previous summer cast shadows across the lawn and spread little pools of light around some of the flowers. With the children's toys cleared away and the rickety den Ruairi had built hidden in the shadows, it all looked very peaceful.

Throwing down the dishcloth she went outside and let the night air cool her overheated face. Maybe this was what she should settle for after all because there was nothing wrong with it, not really. June and Mark always seemed so happy, and so did Peter and Andrew and their wives. Her parents did too. This was the life everyone else in the family seemed to enjoy, so who was she to disparage it? She felt hot with shame as she remembered how often she had criticized everything they had achieved without any thought for their feelings. How could she have been so insensitive? And how could she have forgotten the one thing that made their lives richer by far than anything she might achieve by travelling? How could she have overlooked the love they all had for one another, and which they shared with the wider family? It was the lodestone that kept everything fresh and new, and it was the one thing missing from her own life. She hadn't found it with Graham, which was the real reason she had turned him down, and she wasn't going to find it with Ruairi either because he'd just made that very clear. Love! It was the one thing that all the travel plans in the world would never change.

Then she thought of Jo, of her independence, of her ability to make a home out of nothing, of the matter-of-fact way she had flown home ahead of her husband to organize her confinement, and suddenly she felt diminished. Jo was…she hunted for the word and then stopped abruptly as it came to her. Brave. That was what it was. Jo was brave. She didn't just talk about her plans, she did something about them…she put them into action.

The thought brought self-pitying tears to Maggie's eyes because she didn't think she was very brave and that was only one of her problems. She listed the rest on her fingers: lack of insight, lack of adventure, too much talk and not enough action. And on top of all that, Ruairi had made one thing very clear. Despite their one kiss, there wasn't a place for her in his life, not even via his mother, so she had missed out on love as well. He expected her to live her own life, not follow him, and that was the thought that made her tears flow hard and fast, and which kept her sitting in the garden long after Mark called out that he was off to bed and that she'd better come in before she was bitten to death by mosquitoes.

* * *

Although she had a headache the following morning, Maggie's manner gave no hint of how she was feeling as she threw herself into the preparations for June's homecoming.

By the time Ruairi and Mrs. O'Connor arrived she had already stripped all the beds and the washing machine was chugging away on its third load. Sophie and Amy had helped her to clear away the breakfast things and had then been dispatched to the playroom to tidy away their toys with a promise that they could start cooking as soon as Granny 'Connor arrived.

Mark, after one horrified look at all the activity going on around him, had fled to the calm of his office saying there were some things he had to do before he started his paternity leave.

"Goodness me, what a hive of activity!" Mrs. O'Connor declared as she dumped her bag on a chair, threw her summer coat over the banister, tied one of June's aprons around her middle and started searching through the cupboards for pots and pans.

Maggie met Ruairi's eyes and, despite everything that had passed between them the previous day, they both burst out laughing as they watched his mother take over the kitchen.

"Come on! We're not needed here any longer," he told Maggie. "Let's go shopping."

"I can't yet," she protested. "There's some more washing almost ready to hang out, and

174

I've still got to make up the beds and write a shopping list."

"I'll deal with the washing, you sort the beds," he said. "And you can write the shopping list in the car."

"It's easier to do as he says Maggie because once he has an idea in his mind it's impossible to shift him. Before you go though, can you tell me where June keeps her flour," Mrs. O'Connor resurfaced from her search of the kitchen cupboards, wooden spoon in hand.

* * *

Forty minutes later, still not sure how she had been talked into it, Maggie was adding items to a shopping list while Ruairi overtook a couple of drivers who were looking for parking spaces in the town centre, and turned into a side street.

"As long as you don't mind a short walk there's bound to be a space down here," he said.

"Walking is fine," she stowed the shopping list in her bag. "It'll be good to move a bit faster than child's pace for a change."

He smiled as he slotted the car neatly into a gap between two parked cars and killed the engine. "Are you getting fed up with your domestic responsibilities?"

She shook her head as she opened the passenger door. "Not really. I love the children... it will just be good to stretch my legs."

175

As they set off towards the town centre her hand brushed against Ruairi's. Despite all his good intentions, and without allowing himself to think of the consequences, he seized it and pulled her close to his side. She didn't look at him as she curled her fingers into his. Instead she tried to make a joke of it.

"I'm not Sophie or Amy you know. I can walk safely on my own."

He slowed them both to a stop. "I'm not in any danger of ever confusing you with Sophie or Amy," he said quietly, and then he did the one thing he'd told himself he was never going to do again, he kissed her.

It was a tentative kiss, no more than his lips brushing hers, but this time the connection was immediate. It felt as if a thousand volts had surged through him as she responded, and forgetting they were in a quiet suburban street, he let her soft lips become his whole focus. For what seemed to be a very long time they explored one another's mouths, their breathing erratic as they pressed against one another, the fact that they were on a public street the only thing that stopped their feverish hands from roaming across bodies suddenly hot with desire. Ruairi didn't come to his senses until a couple of teenage boys cycling past made ribald comments. When he heard them he drew back from Maggie with a wry smile.

"I'm sorry," he said. "I didn't mean that to happen."

Her face was flushed, her lips still slightly parted as she looked up at him.

"I know you didn't," she said, her voice and her gaze steady. "I know you are going away again Ruairi, and I know there won't be a place for me in your life when you do but…but can't we pretend it's not like that, just for today."

At a complete loss for words, he stared down at her. She was keeping whatever was going on inside her head to herself. All he could see reflected in her wide grey eyes were his own feelings of desire and frustration. It brought him to his senses and, his heart heavy, he shook his head.

"You know it doesn't work like that Maggie. If we take today, then we'll want tomorrow too, and the day after that."

"And would that really be so terrible," she whispered, her face pale now, her body rigid in the circle of his arms.

"Yes, because then I'd break your heart," he said, letting his hands drop to his sides. "I'm always on the move, always away. And when I'm home I'm still distracted half the time, organizing new contracts, working on documentaries. I don't have time for a relationship Maggie. These few days have been a real time out for me, and I've enjoyed them and being with you more than I can say, but they're nearly over. After my meeting tomorrow I'll probably be away for months and what sort of life would that be for you. You deserve far more than that and I should never have taken advantage of you."

To his surprise her eyes blazed gray fire at him. "It didn't feel to me like you were taking advantage. It takes two you know. If I hadn't wanted to kiss you then I wouldn't have."

He caught her arm as she turned away and began to walk towards the town centre. "I didn't mean this...I'm not talking about now. I meant I should have walked away the first moment I knew I wanted you. Instead, I told myself that playing happy families with you for a few days would be fun and that we were both too grown up to get carried away by our emotions."

"Well now you know you were wrong don't you! But if you still want to play happy families and help me finish this shopping, then that's fine by me. I'll try not to let my emotions get in the way." She wrenched her arm away from him and began to stride out in earnest.

He hurried to catch up with her. "I know I deserve that and worse, and I'm sorry, but please wait Maggie. Let's talk about this some more. We can't let our friendship end like this."

They reached the end of the street as he finished speaking but whatever Maggie was going to say to him in reply was never uttered because someone called out to them. It was Jenny, Peter's wife. Barely looking both ways she rushed across the street towards them, dodging a passing car.

"Hello you two. Mrs. O'Connor said I might bump into you both. She said you had

178

gone shopping when I called to see how you were getting on with the children Maggie."

"Everything's fine," there wasn't a tremor in Maggie's voice as she smiled at her. "We have a long list of things we need to get for June's homecoming though. Have you heard that she and the baby are both being discharged tomorrow?"

"Yes, I did. Isn't it great? Have you bought anything for him yet?"

"No. It's one of the things on my list, well it's several really because I need to buy him something from the girls, and Mrs. O'Connor has asked me to find a gift for her to give to June too."

"Let's go together then," Jenny linked arms with her as they walked towards the shopping centre. "If we do then we won't end up duplicating things. Is that okay with you Ruairi?" she asked, twisting her head round to smile at him.

"Don't mind me. I'm just here to carry the bags," he said.

* * *

The rest of the morning passed swiftly. By the time Maggie and Jenny had chosen baby clothes and toys for their new nephew, it was nearly lunchtime. Declaring that she and Ruairi had to hurry back to give the children lunch, Maggie kissed her sister-in-law goodbye and then, with Ruairi following, made a whistle-stop

179

tour of the local supermarket to collect the various items she needed to decorate the cake and cater for the welcome home party.

She didn't speak to him at all until they were standing in the checkout queue and even then she kept the conversation on everyday matters, talking about how excited Sophie and Amy would be to have their mother at home again, and wondering how soon they would get over the novelty of having a new baby brother.

Ruairi, taking his cue from her, agreed with everything she said even though all he wanted to do was to sweep her into his arms in the middle of the supermarket and tell her he was sorry, sorry, sorry. Sorry for leading her on when there was no future for them; sorry for taking advantage of her; and most of all, sorry he had to say goodbye.

He didn't though. Instead, he dutifully unloaded the items from the trolley onto the checkout counter while she packed the shopping, and then he picked up the bags and carried them to where he had parked the car. Once they were back at Mark's house he helped her to unload everything and then carried all the bags into a kitchen that smelled deliciously of baking, and dumped them on the counter.

"Did you get sweeties to decorate the cake?" demanded Sophie.

"I think so. You'd better ask Auntie Maggie," he told her, suddenly feeling very weary.

"Are you alright Ruairi?" His mother turned around from where she was stirring a casserole and looked at him.

"He's absolutely fine," said Maggie, walking into the kitchen and bending down to hug first Sophie and then Amy. "He just didn't realize what hard work it was going to be playing happy families, did you Ruairi?"

* * *

The rest of the day was a whirl of activity as, with Mrs. O'Connor's help, the girls iced and then decorated the cake, made welcome home cards and then, with Maggie supervising, colored in the long WELCOME HOME banner she had bought for them. By the time Ruairi had tacked it over the front door and then blown up at least twenty balloons and tied them to the porch, they were beside themselves with excitement.

"Let's put up that fluffy sparkle too," said Amy. "The Christmas one," she added when nobody seemed to know what she was talking about.

"Oh, you mean tinsel," Maggie laughed. "Well I don't see why not. It would make everything look extra special wouldn't it?"

"Yes! Yes!" Both little girls rushed over to Ruairi. "It's in Daddy's shed," they told him.

"Well you'd better show me where," he said, keeping his voice as cheerful and enthusiastic as Maggie's had been the whole of the afternoon.

Mrs. O'Connor looked across at Maggie as he followed the little girls into the garden. "Is something the matter Maggie? Have you and Ruairi had a quarrel?"

"Goodness me, whatever makes you think that? I can't imagine what we could possibly fall out about?" Maggie busied herself filling the kettle, hoping as she did so that her voice didn't sound as brittle to Mrs. O'Connor's ears as it did to her own.

* * *

For once Maggie was pleased when it was time for Ruairi and his mother to leave. They had greeted June when Mark brought her and the baby home from the hospital and had shared in the celebrations too, declaring the inexpertly iced cake with its covering of brightly colored sweets to be delicious. Although she had then invited them to stay to supper she was relieved when they refused.

"I've had a lovely day," Mrs. O'Connor said, giving her a hug. "And you chose just the right present for the baby. That little jacket is really cute and I'll enjoy seeing him wearing it when he's a little older."

Maggie returned her hug, promising to see her again very soon. Then she turned to Ruairi.

"Good luck at your interview tomorrow," she said.

He searched her face. She was giving nothing away. "Thank you."

They walked to the front door, the girls and Mrs. O'Connor in front, all three of them chattering away, Ruairi level with Maggie. He looked at her.

"Still friends?" he asked.

She hesitated for just a moment. Then she turned and looked up at him, her grey eyes curiously opaque.

"Still friends," she replied.

Chapter Fourteen

Thanks to an endless stream of visitors Maggie had little time to think now June and the baby were home from hospital. She was kept busy making cups of tea and coffee when she wasn't helping Sophie and Amy to display the growing pile of congratulatory cards that arrived with every post, or putting away the many small garments friends and family brought for baby John. The rest of her time was spent keeping the main part of the house as tidy as possible as well as coping with the extra washing and ironing, and cooking meals for all of them whilst continuing to keep an eye on the children.

"You've been wonderful Maggie," June said to her in one of the rare moments they were alone together. "I can't begin to imagine how we would have managed without you and I'm just so sorry that I can't do more to help at the moment."

"Don't you dare to even try," Maggie told her. "You're still recovering from an emergency caesarian in case you've forgotten, and the shock and worry of John's first few days as well. Besides, Mum would never forgive me if I left you and Mark to cope by yourselves before she arrives home."

"I know," June's smile of agreement suddenly became mischievous. "Although maybe I've been doing you a favor anyway because if everything I've been hearing is true, then you've had the gorgeous Ruairi O'Connor helping you day and night while I've been in hospital!"

"You always did talk nonsense," Maggie replied, managing to hide her face by turning away to rearrange the huge bouquet of flowers that had arrived an hour or so earlier.

"These are lovely. And what a wonderful surprise to receive them from your parents with a message saying they're coming over to see you in a couple of month's time."

"Mmm." Although June was indeed delighted with the flowers and the fact she would soon be able to show her new son to her parents, right now moment she was much too concerned about Maggie to play along with her attempt to change the subject."

"Maggie, tell me what's the matter? Have you had an argument with Ruairi?" She knew if it was something to do with Mark or the children her sister-in-law would have told her by now, so it must be Ruairi.

When Maggie continued to keep her back turned towards her she knew she was right. Something had happened between them. She remembered seeing them together at the ruby wedding and feeling sure a romance would follow, so when Mark and the children had kept mentioning Ruairi and she had realized how

185

much time he was spending with Maggie, she'd been delighted. She had never thought Maggie was ready to settle down with Mark's friend Graham, even though he was meant to be such a paragon. To her he had always seemed far too staid for her mercurial sister-in-law whereas someone like Ruairi O'Connor was exactly the sort of person June would have chosen for her.

Maggie had always been her favorite member of the Silver family, ever since she had first met her. She remembered going home with Mark to meet his parents and being entranced by the slim red-haired girl who was so eager for life, and who had constantly bombarded her with questions about Australia. Maggie had been in her early teens then; still at school, but with big plans for the future, plans she had shared with June but which had somehow failed to materialize once she left school. Instead she had continued to live at home and had settled for a local job as a primary school teacher. For the first time, June wondered what had happened.

"Maggie if there's a problem, please let me help. Remember how you used to tell me everything once upon a time?

"Ruairi *is* the problem!" Maggie stopped fiddling with the flowers and turned and faced her. Although June was shocked by the bleakness of her expression she didn't comment. Instead she waited.

"I still have a crush on him, except it's not a just a crush any longer. I'm in love with him,"

Maggie blurted out. "I can't help it June. The feeling won't go away and it…it hurts…and I don't know what to do."

"And Ruairi?" June's voice was gentle because she could see Maggie was close to tears.

"That's what's so terrible. Ruairi feels the same. At first I didn't think he did, but now I know he does. He just won't allow himself to give in to it. He says the life he leads would make me unhappy. He says he spends so much time travelling that we would barely see one another. He says I deserve something better."

June heard the catch in her voice and her heart went out to her. "And you've been dealing with all this while you've been looking after Sophie and Amy. Oh Maggie, I'm so sorry. Are you sure there's no way you can get him to change his mind?"

"Not when he's off on his travels again in a couple of weeks, I can't. There's just no time June. I know I need to forget him and start to plan my own life, and once Mum comes home and takes over here that's what I'm going to do," she added, scrubbing at her eyes.

Then they heard the front door open. It was Mark returning from a trip to the local shops with the children. Maggie lowered her voice. "You won't tell Mark or any of the rest of them though, will you? Promise. Please promise."

Her eyes were wide with pleading as she looked at her sister-in-law. June shook her head, wishing there was some way she could solve Maggie's problem.

"I promise."

* * *

Ruairi didn't call Maggie after his interview with the Production Company. He phoned Jo though and told her that everything had been agreed. He'd also managed to delay his Mexican contract, which meant he could return to New Zealand immediately.

"I just need to get Mum back to Ireland and then I'll be on my way," he said.

"Maggie will miss you. Have you told her when you're leaving?" Jo had already been to see June and the baby, and the two women had bonded in more ways than one as they discussed Australia, living far away from family, the joys of having children of their own and then, at the end, just before Jo left, Maggie.

Remembering that Maggie had only sworn her to secrecy as far as her own family was concerned; June pushed away a feeling of guilt as she conveyed her worries about Maggie's state of mind to Jo. After that it had taken very little for Jo to admit that she was just as concerned about Ruairi.

"He drives himself too hard," she said. "I've known him for a long time and he's always been the same. Partly it's passion for his work of course, but there's more to it than that. It's as if by working every moment he's awake he can make sure he doesn't have time to stop and think. That's why I was amazed at how he was when he met me at the airport with Maggie and the children. I don't think I've ever seen him so relaxed, and he was good with Sophie and Amy too, but now that he's off to New Zealand again he seems to have reverted to type. "

So now, without giving anything away about the conversation she'd had with June, Jo was quizzing him about Maggie. And each word she spoke was like a sharp blade twisting in his heart. For a moment he was tempted to talk to her, to tell her how he felt about Maggie, and why he was so sure he had to leave her behind to live her own life. Then he squashed the urge. Sharing his pain wouldn't make it any better. He finished the conversation as swiftly as he could without answering any of her questions.

As she slowly replaced the handset Jo was thoughtful. Ruairi had always been such a good friend to her and Ollie that she wanted him to be as happy as they were. And if his happiness meant that he and Maggie needed a couple of fairy godmothers then she was just going to have to dust off her wand and persuade June to do the same.

* * *

Maggie didn't know a thing about Ruairi's leaving date, or even if the production company had accepted his documentary idea until he brought Mrs. O'Connor to visit June and the new baby again. She was laden with gifts and flowers, as well as a bottle of Scotch for Mark.

"It's to thank you for being so welcoming, Mrs. O'Connor told him when he protested. "Now let me give baby John a cuddle before Sophie and Amy realize we're here and try to drag me away to play with them."

Maggie was in the kitchen with the children who were helping her make the pastry she was going to use for an apple pie for lunchtime dessert. With the door closed and Sophie and Amy chattering non-stop as they kneaded their own very grey looking balls of dough, she didn't realize they had visitors until she looked up and saw Ruairi standing in the doorway.

The lurch her heart gave at the sight of him temporarily removed her power of speech. Ruairi seemed to be having a similar problem until the children, full of excitement that he had reappeared in their lives again, held up their uncooked pastry balls for inspection. Somehow he managed to admire them and ask what they were making while maintaining eye contact with Maggie.

"How are you?" he asked.

"Never better," she told him. "Busy though. Ever since June and John came home the house has been full of visitors bringing presents for the baby and flowers for June."

"All of which has meant a lot of work for Maggie," said Mark as he came into the kitchen to fill the kettle. "Why don't you go in and see Mrs. O'Connor, while I make coffee for us all."

Maggie didn't need a second invitation. She would do anything to avoid being alone with Ruairi again. Swiftly wrapping the pastry in cling film she put it in the fridge, rinsed her hands under the tap, and then followed the children through to the sitting room where Mrs. O'Connor was cuddling the sleeping baby.

"There you are my dears," she said, her face lighting up at the sight of Maggie and the children. Then, before Sophie and Amy could disturb John by coming too close, she stood up and settled him in his crib. Once she was certain he was going to stay asleep, she hugged them.

"Now if you two girls can help me to open the bags I've left by the door, there are presents for all of you."

"For Auntie Maggie too?" asked Sophie as she darted across the room.

"Certainly for Auntie Maggie too. Hers is the big one."

Mystified, Maggie slowly unwrapped the bulky present while Mrs. O'Connor helped the children to unwrap theirs. Inside the layers of blue paper was a flight bag made of soft, burgundy-colored leather, and when she opened it she found a matching document case inside with sections for travel documents, insurance papers, passport, credit cards; everything a traveler might need to carry.

"It's beautiful," she said, stroking the soft leather. "But you really shouldn't have bought me anything at all, let alone something as expensive as this."

"Nonsense! You've made me so welcome and encouraged me to start to plan for the future too, instead of wallowing in the past, so this is my way of saying thank you. I'm so pleased you like it though because I must admit I wouldn't have thought of buying it for you myself. It was Ruairi's idea. He said it's just what you need to get you started on your travels."

Maggie kept smiling as she hugged and thanked Mrs. O'Connor and then admired the presents she had bought for the children. She wouldn't let herself weep the bitter tears that were pricking the back of her eyelids, or acknowledge the fact that Ruairi's choice of gift had finally made her realize, more than anything else had, that there was no future with him at all. He was going back to his own life and the beautiful burgundy luggage was his message to her. He expected her to do the same as him. He expected her to pick up her travel plans when she had finished looking after June, and to make a life for herself, the life she had once told him about before her dreams went sour.

She kept smiling right through the visit and when Mrs. O'Connor hugged her goodbye, she promised to visit her in Ireland. She even let Ruairi give her a farewell kiss on the cheek after he had done the same to June and to the children, and shaken Mark by the hand. Then, as they gathered in the doorway to wave them off, she aimed for a lighthearted exit line.

"Good luck with your documentary. And let us know when it's going to be broadcast so we can tell everyone we know the famous Ruairi O'Connor who made it."

It drew the laugh she was aiming for, so that the last view Ruairi had of her was her smiling face before she turned away and went indoors, back to her pastry. The fact that the apple pie she was making turned out to be a complete failure was blamed on an uncharacteristic absent-mindedness on Maggie's part. After all, why else would she have forgotten to add sugar to the apples, and why else would she have burnt the pastry almost to a crisp?

Only June, trying to salvage a few edible mouthfuls, failed to join in with the teasing laughter. Instead, she studied Maggie's face and noticed a faint pinkness around her eyes that she hadn't quite managed to conceal with extra eyeliner and mascara.

Chapter Fifteen

Cathy and John Silver returned home a few days later, tanned and relaxed and desperate to see their latest grandchild. Once he had been proclaimed perfect, and June and Mark had been congratulated for the umpteenth time, and Sophie and Amy had been hugged and kissed and cuddled, Cathy Silver turned her attention to Maggie.

"You're looking a bit peaky dear," she told her. "All this domesticity seems to have worn you out. Never mind. I'm here now so you can get back to your own life."

Maggie knew that she didn't mean to be unkind but it still rankled. Why did her mother have to be so dismissive? Why did she never give her any credit? Only June's fervent thanks for all she had done soothed her as she collected her belongings together, ready to go home.

"I'll drive you," her Dad said, picking up her small suitcase.

"No, don't bother. I'd rather walk. I could do with the fresh air." Maggie was suddenly very anxious to leave. She needed some time on her own before she had to face her mother's inquisition about everything that had happened while she'd been away.

"Well in that case we'll just bring your suitcase back with us when we come home." Her father sank down into his armchair again, obviously relieved that he didn't have to make an extra car journey.

"Would you cuddle your new grandson while the girls and I say goodbye to Maggie," June's usually gentle manner was slightly acerbic as she thrust the baby at her mother-in-law before following Maggie out of the room. When they reached the front door they stopped.

"Kiss Auntie Maggie goodbye children," she instructed Sophie and Amy. "And thank her for looking after you for so long."

Both children flung their arms around Maggie's neck as she knelt down to their level. "We love you," said Sophie, while Amy gently rubbed Maggie's cheek with pink rabbit."

"And I love you too," tears sprang to Maggie's eyes as she hugged them. She scrubbed them away as she got to her feet. "Stupid of me," she told June.

"Not stupid at all! Now go home and have a long, hot bath with lots of bubbles, and relax. And try to forget what your mother said too. You know she doesn't mean it."

"I know," Maggie gave her the ghost of a smile. "It's just that sometimes it would be nice to know she thought I could do something right."

* * *

Things got back to normal pretty quickly after that. Thanks to all the support she'd received, June recovered swiftly and soon took over the reins of her household again although she was grateful for the extra help Cathy Silver continued to give her on an almost daily basis.

John Silver Senior returned to his final year at work so brown and relaxed from his cruise that his work colleagues teasingly told him he looked as if he had already retired so maybe they would cancel the farewell retirement party they were arranging for him.

Mark finished his paternity leave and hurried back to his office with a mixture of relief and regret, but not before June had made him promise he would take Sophie to school and Amy to nursery every morning once the new term started. He also agreed that he wouldn't stay late at the office.

Sophie and Amy soon forgot that baby John was a new member of the family and treated him as if he had always been there, sometimes cuddling him, sometimes forgetting about him for hours at a time when friends came to play, or when their grandmother took them to the park.

Maggie made preparations for the start of the autumn term and the class of new children she would have to teach. She went shopping, too, and bought some new slacks and a couple of jumpers to smarten up her work wardrobe. She even started to trawl the internet again in a half-hearted attempt to find a teaching contract in another country. She buried her beautiful new flight bag at the very back of her wardrobe though, so she wouldn't have to look at it on a daily basis. There was one other thing too. She stopped smiling, and very soon everyone started to notice.

"Whatever is the matter with you?" her Mother asked her in exasperation on one of the rare evenings when Maggie ate with her parents. "You've hardly spoken to us since we returned from our cruise, and whenever we see you, you look as if you have all the worries of the world on your shoulders when in actual fact you've hardly any responsibilities at all."

Her father didn't ask questions. Instead he buried himself behind his daily paper or turned on the Sports Channel whenever Maggie was around, but he did send a worried glance in her direction every now and again when he thought she wasn't looking.

As for her brothers, they tried to jolly her out of it by telling her that not wanting to go back to work after a long holiday was all part of growing up; that if she had agreed to get engaged to Graham when he proposed to her then she would have had something to look forward to by now instead of indulging in the miseries; that maybe she should take up jogging or something else energetic to get her blood flowing or, instead, become a volunteer and help people who had real problems, instead of sitting at home feeling sorry for herself.

Only Mark got close to the truth when he teased her about Ruairi, saying he supposed that now he had returned to New Zealand she didn't have anyone to discuss her so called travel plans with.

Maggie ignored them all. She tried to ignore the fact that she was missing Ruairi too, but that was like trying to ignore a missing tooth, especially when everyone around her seemed to be conspiring to keep him in the forefront of her mind, making her probe her memories of their time together, the memory of kissing him. First it was her mother, reading a letter from Mrs. O'Connor at the breakfast table.

"She says to give you her love," she told Maggie, after relaying the fact that she was serious about moving back to England, especially now that Ruairi was away again.

"He's gone back to New Zealand to work on a documentary and she doesn't know when he'll be home again," she said. "Did you know about that? Did you know he was going to leave his poor mother alone again?" she asked Maggie accusingly.

Maggie didn't bother to answer because a reply wasn't necessary. Instead she resigned herself to listening to her mother's views about an only son who thought nothing of abandoning his poor widowed mother in the middle of nowhere.

"That's hardly fair, dear," John Silver observed mildly from behind his newspaper. "After all he left home years ago and the O'Connors made their own decision to move to Ireland long after he left."

"That's as may be…" Cathy Silver was getting ready to air her views on family life and responsibilities when Maggie, unable to take any more, pushed back her chair and, making her excuses, fled from the table.

Next she had to admire the postcards Ruairi had sent the children and agree they were the best pictures of penguins she'd ever seen, while all the time her heart was reminding her that he had also sent postcards to her when she was a child. It was only now she was an adult that he was ignoring her.

June earned her eternal gratitude by not mentioning Ruairi at all but, instead, handing her baby John so she could cuddle him, and then asking her about her own plans for the future.

"You know you can always go and visit my parents for a while if you need a change of scene," she said. "They would love to see you. Why don't you ask them when they get here?"

"Mmm," Maggie was non-committal but the more she toyed with the idea, the more sensible it seemed. She even broached it to Jo when she made one of her regular visits to see her.

"Sounds good to me," Jo was enthusiastic. "It would be a great way to get your first experience of long distance travel but with a safety net at the end of it. You'd probably be able to find some sort of short-term job too, just to give you a taste of working in a different country.

Maggie looked at her new friend. Jo was a lot more pregnant now but she still appeared to be quite calm about living on her own, and was preparing for her forthcoming baby in between writing papers about the work she and Ollie were doing in New Zealand.

"You didn't need a safety net," she said.

"Oh yes I did!" Jo laughed as she settled herself into the chair opposite. "When I first started travelling on my own I probably called my poor mother every single day. It cost her a fortune in reverse phone charges, and I had been brought up to travel the globe whereas you…"

"Have never been anywhere," Maggie finished for her.

"I wasn't going to say that," Jo's voice was gentle, and if Maggie had looked she would have seen real concern in her eyes. "I was just going to say that as you are still trying to decide what you want to do maybe a long term teaching job in another country is not the best starting point, whereas I had my career all cut and dried by the time I was in my teens."

"Lucky you!"

"Lucky me indeed. But not many people know what they want to do at such an early age. Did you always want to be a primary school teacher or is it something that just happened?"

Maggie was thoughtful as she replied. "I guess it sort of crept up on me. I like children and I was always good with them because I've had a lot of practice with all my nieces and nephews, but apart from that…well I didn't

200

have any better ideas once I finished university, not realistic ones anyway. "

Then she surprised herself by telling Jo about her real dreams for the future. The ones she'd never shared with anyone since the day her parents had dismissed them as pie in the sky and told her she needed to get herself a proper job, one that came with a career structure and a pension.

"Eventually I'd like to write books for children, fact and fiction, and illustrate them, but I'm unlikely to ever earn enough to keep myself by doing that, I'm just concentrating on my teaching career at the moment."

"But you're not letting that stop you surely?" Jo looked genuinely shocked. "Please tell me that you are writing and painting in your spare time."

Maggie flushed with embarrassment. "Well…no. I mean, I did start…I do have a lot of stuff stored away…but somehow I've let life get in the way. You must think I'm a real failure," she added miserably.

"Failure? No, of course I don't. But I do think you make yourself far too available to your family. Tell me, why do you still live with your parents?"

It wasn't possible for Maggie's cheeks to flush any pinker as she searched for a reply. "Well I don't really live with them even though it looks that way. I have my own space, my own bathroom and sitting room as well as a bedroom. It's just that when Mum said it was silly for me to live in a bedsit when they had plenty of room at home, it seemed a bit churlish to refuse," she finished lamely.

"I guess," Jo nodded understandingly although she didn't make any further comment. Instead she changed the subject.

"Ollie arrives home on Saturday!"

"How fantastic! I didn't realize he was coming so soon. You must be really excited. What time does he arrive? Would you like me to drive you to the airport to meet him?"

Maggie was so thrilled for her friend that she pushed her own unhappiness to the back of her mind.

Jo shook her head. "I couldn't ask you to do that Maggie. It would take a big chunk out of the middle of your day. Besides, I was thinking of hiring a car."

"But you don't need to, not when I don't have any other plans. I'd be happy to take you, honestly."

"Well if you're really sure then I must admit I'd be glad of the company. I'm beginning to feel a bit nervous about travelling too far on my own now that I've only a couple of weeks to go."

"Is it really that soon?" Maggie looked at the very pregnant mound of Jo's stomach with interest.

"I'm afraid so but I have no intention of having this baby until Ollie is well and truly home. I've learned to cope with being apart for months at a time, and with him being so absorbed in what he's doing when he's around that he barely speaks for days on end, but I have no intention of coping with childbirth without him!"

Maggie smiled at her. "I think I would feel the same. I think you're marvelous to have coped with living alone over here for as long as you have."

* * *

The journey to the airport took longer than Maggie had anticipated owing to a minor accident blocking off two lanes of the highway. To make sure Jo didn't miss Ollie, she stopped at the drop off point.

"You go on inside in case the flight has landed early. I'll park the car and come and find you."

Jo didn't need telling twice. She almost fell out of the car in her eagerness to find her husband and barely gave Maggie a backward glance as she hurried into the airport. Suppressing a twinge of envy, Maggie found the entrance to the short stay car park and drove up a series of ramps until she found a parking space. Then, having secured her car and collected a parking token, she made her way through to the Arrivals Hall where she knew Jo would be waiting.

She arrived just as Ollie came through the double doors onto the airport concourse. She knew it was him without being told because he was pushing a trolley laden with a huge rucksack as well as various pieces of bulky equipment packed in sturdy canvas bags which had then been secured with tape and bubble wrap. He also had the same out-of-doors look that Ruairi had, as well as the tan. He didn't look anything like the man in the wedding photograph though. He was sporting a curly black beard and wearing the sort of sleeveless jacket she imagined explorers wore, one that was full of pockets and zips, and which bulged with unseen objects.

His face lit up when he saw Jo and without bothering to walk around the barrier towards her, he abandoned his trolley, leaned across the space between them and kissed her very slowly and very thoroughly, much to the amusement of everyone around them.

Maggie's fragile heart gave a funny little thud and then another when she saw the happiness on Jo's face. If that was what absence did for them, then maybe there was something to be said for it. Not that she would ever know of course because Ruairi had made it very clear he wasn't about to take chances on that sort of love. For him work came first, last and always, and she didn't have any say in the matter.

Forcing her lips into a smile she waved when she saw Jo looking for her, and soon she had been introduced to Ollie and the three of them were making their way back to where she had parked the car.

"This is so kind of you," Ollie said as he fitted his luggage into the trunk. "And so is everything else you've done for Jo. She told me all about it when we talked on the webcam, and Ruairi has spoken about you too."

"Is he...I mean how is his work going?" Maggie asked, hoping he hadn't noticed her blush when he mentioned Ruairi's name.

"Fine I think. We haven't talked about it much. Both too busy I guess!" He smiled down at her, keeping his expression neutral. He had no intention of telling her that Ruairi appeared to be suffering from a severe bout of lovesickness because, according to Jo, it would apparently be more than his life was worth if he told Maggie anything at all; and after leaving his wife to fend for herself for almost two months he had every intention of doing exactly what she told him.

* * *

Much later, after she had delivered Ollie and Jo to their flat and tried very hard not to envy them their obvious happiness, Maggie drove home and sat for a long time in her car, thinking.

When she eventually let herself into the house there was nobody in. With a sigh of relief she hurried through to the part of the house that was hers and closed the door firmly behind her. Now she would be able to put her plan into operation without having to answer her mother's inevitable questions.

Kicking off her shoes, she changed into her oldest jeans and then climbed the narrow flight of stairs that led up to the attic. As she pushed open the door she was assailed by the musty smell of things that had been stored for a very long time. She wrinkled her nose as she switched on the overhead light. All around her was the debris of family life; broken chairs, old curtains that would never be hung again, bags of clothes waiting to be taken to a charity shop, piles of dusty books, even school bags and old footballs and cricket bats despite the fact her brothers had all left home years ago. And there, behind it all, hidden deep in an old tea chest where she had put them several years before, were Maggie's manuscripts and paintings.

Pulling them out, she sank down on the floor and leafed through them. They were better than she had remembered. Not good enough of course, but still good.

Don't waste your talent one of her tutors had told her when she was at university and he had seen her work. *You've got what it takes Maggie. You've just got to believe in yourself.*

"And yet I've done exactly the opposite," she whispered, covering her face with her hands. "I've wasted my talent. I've stopped believing in myself and listened to other people instead. Well it's not going to happen anymore!"

She dusted herself off, gathered up the papers as well as a large box of paints and brushes and made her way downstairs, back to her small sitting room. Once there she spread the paintings out on the table and stared at them for a very long time before carefully stacking them into two separate piles. Then she fired up her laptop computer, opened a new file, and typed in the words Children's Book.

For a long time after that Maggie was busy. Lost in her own world she forgot to eat supper. She didn't hear her parents return home either and when hunger and thirst eventually drove her to the kitchen it was dark and quiet outside, and her mother and father were both sound asleep in bed.

Chapter Sixteen

Autumn arrived with an extra burst of sunshine that lifted everyone's spirits as they settled back into their usual routine. Even Maggie's gloom lifted because although the feeling of loss Ruairi had left behind didn't go away, she soon found she was able to push it to the back of her mind for hours at a time while she worked on her children's book.

With all her nieces and nephews back at school, no family occasion looming, and her mother preoccupied with her latest grandson, she was able to spend every spare moment either tapping away at her computer or working on a series of illustrations for the book she had in mind. She didn't share her secret with anyone, not even Jo. Nor did she correct her family's assumption that she was preparing lessons or correcting class homework when she shut herself in her room.

She still managed to visit June and the children though; and Jo as soon as she had her baby, a little boy who she named Henry, and who arrived on time and healthy.

"He's absolutely gorgeous," she told her as she laid flowers, a card and a present on the hospital locker next to the bed.

"He is, isn't he?" Jo grinned at her. "And I managed to hold onto him until Ollie came home."

Maggie looked down at the little boy who was fast asleep in his hospital cot. His head was covered in fluffy curls and he had screwed his tiny pink face into a ferocious frown. She leaned forward and lifted one of his hands. It looked like a miniature starfish against her palm.

"Have you told Ruairi about him," she asked before she could stop herself.

"Of course. Ollie emailed him straight away and told him to try to get back here to see him before he starts kindergarten!"

Maggie laughed, as she knew Jo meant her to, but deep inside the hurt that was always with her bloomed and grew at the sight of the tiny baby in the cot. There was something about Henry that moved her in a way that her own nieces and nephews never had.

"Would you like to hold him?" Jo's eyes were wide with compassion as she watched her. "He's due to wake for a feed shortly so it doesn't matter if you disturb him."

Maggie didn't need a second invitation. She bent down and lifted Henry to her shoulder, breathing in talc and baby lotion and an ineffable baby smell that went straight to her heart. She knew the connection she felt with Henry was because of Ruairi and she tried hard not to feel bitter because he had not been ready take a chance on the sort of love that had produced this tiny replica of Ollie.

Blinking away the tears that were pricking her eyelids, she pressed her lips to Henry's downy head and her heart contracted as she felt him snuggle into the warm hollow of her neck. Adjusting him more comfortably against her chest she turned back to Jo.

"How long before you take him back to New Zealand?"

"Didn't I tell you? We've wangled a pass to stay here until at least the middle of next year because Ollie managed to complete enough research in the last couple of months he was there to keep him busy at the computer for quite a while."

"Oh Jo, I'm so glad!" As Henry started to wriggle Maggie held him away from her shoulder so she could look at him. His eyes were open and he peered up at her like a grumpy old man. Then he screwed up his face and started to cry.

"I guess I'm not the person he needs right at this moment," she said as she reluctantly handed him over to his mother.

* * *

Later that evening, back in her room, she sat and stared out of the window for almost an hour. Then she opened a second file on her computer and labeled it. This time she typed in Children's Book 2: New Baby.

* * *

Life continued uninterrupted until the middle of October when an unseasonal squall chased the leaves off the trees earlier than usual. Maggie spent her mid-term vacation researching publishing houses and writing letters of introduction that outlined her ideas. She knew she would be lucky to receive any sort of response so she was pleasantly surprised a few weeks later when one of the smaller publishers replied asking her to send in some samples of her work.

Bogged down at school by Christmas concerts and carol services, and busy at home helping her mother prepare for the major undertaking that was the Silver family's Christmas dinner, she didn't have time to immediately do as they asked, and she knew it would have to wait until the New Year. Nevertheless the thought of it stayed with her while she made batches of mince pies for the freezer, and when she stayed after work to help decorate the school hall ready for the concert. And it was with her when she went Christmas shopping, and when she decorated the oversized Christmas tree that her father insisted on buying every year. It even stayed with her when the usual family dispute erupted about who would be visiting whom over the holiday period.

Nothing fazed her as she hugged the possibility of success close. Nothing, that is, until the Christmas cards started to arrive. Mrs. O'Connor's was one of the first to plop onto the doormat and Maggie opened it with trepidation. As she had anticipated, the envelope contained a letter as well as a card. She wanted to ignore it because she didn't want to think about Ruairi. Since he had left for New Zealand she had managed to regain some of her equanimity, and although keeping busy had been part of it, not seeing him and not talking about him had been just as important. Now, with Mrs. O'Connor's letter, she was going to have to look her despair in the face again. With trembling fingers she unfolded the page.

Dear Maggie

I can't believe almost four months has gone by since I had that lovely holiday in England. I've been very busy since then. Ruairi bought me a laptop computer before he returned to New Zealand, and he set it up for me and taught me how to browse the internet. He showed me how to use the webcam too, so now I can talk to him and see him at the same time. It's wonderful! I don't know why I didn't have one before. It makes him seem so much closer. And he shows me things too, now that we can see one another, so I'm beginning to understand much more about his work.

I've even been using the internet to search for somewhere to live in England and I think I've found exactly what I've been looking for. I'm coming over to see it in the New Year, and if I like it and manage to buy it, then I will only be a short bus ride away from you and your parents.

Anyway that's enough for now my dear. I hope that your own plans are coming on well. You will be able to tell me all about them when I fly over to look at the bungalow I've found. In fact I would love you to visit it with me if you have the time.

Happy Christmas and I'll see you in the New Year

Love Moira O'Connor

Maggie let the letter rest in her lap as she stared out of the window at the darkening sky. So Mrs. O'Connor was definitely going to move back to England. Well that was good. She needed to be back with her friends. What was not so good was the fact she would have to talk about Ruairi whenever she met her. She might even have to meet him again on the rare occasions he came home, and she wasn't at all sure she would be able to cope with that.

Her mother interrupted her thoughts as she popped her head around the door of Maggie's sitting room.

"Oh there you are dear. Please come and help me wrap the Christmas presents. There are so many of them I haven't got the time to sit down and rest, even if you have."

She turned and hurried away without waiting to see if she was following her. Maggie sighed as she got to her feet. Her mother could be so irritating and yet there was a warm heart beating underneath all that bossiness and criticism. If only she could be persuaded to loosen the reins that bound the Silver family then she would enjoy her life far more. The problem was that she worried about everything, and when she worried, she fussed. Maggie knew it was the reason she was being particularly hard on her at the moment. Ever since she'd turned down Graham's proposal her mother had been in a permanent state of worry. She couldn't envisage one of her children living a life different from her own. She wanted them settled and content, and living as close to her as was possible, so she was worried that Maggie wanted to travel and work in another country; worried that she spent so much time shut up in her room; worried that she had turned down a perfectly good proposal of marriage and didn't seem to be interested in finding another boyfriend. The list was endless.

Maggie knew all this, and as she made her way into the dining room where her mother was wrestling with wrapping paper and tape, she suddenly realized with surprise that it didn't bother her anymore. Losing Ruairi, seeing June and Mark cope with the traumatic birth of baby John, meeting Jo and Ollie and learning from them that there were other ways to live, all these things had conspired to make her grow up.

In four short months she had changed from someone who took every critical remark to heart, to a person who had learned to look outside herself and see things from a very different perspective.

"Before I help you with the presents, I'm going to make you a cup of tea," she told her mother with a smile. "So instead of struggling on your own, why don't you put your feet up for a few minutes and read the paper, or listen to some music. Then we'll do it together. You need to have a rest Mum, otherwise you'll be too worn out to enjoy Christmas."

Her mother sank back on the chair, her eyes wide with surprise. Then she slowly nodded her head. "I know you're right Maggie. I just never seem to relax enough to stop."

"Well now's the time," Maggie said. "I'll be back in a few minutes with tea and biscuits and then maybe we should make a list of everything else that needs to be done before Christmas."

* * *

Drinking the tea while they drew up a 'to do' list together proved to be a turning point for Maggie and her mother, and by the time Christmas arrived Cathy Silver was telling anyone who would listen that she didn't know how she would have managed to get everything ready without Maggie.

Impressed, her brothers teased her less and took her more seriously, even asking her about her travel plans without a hint of sarcasm in their voices. And when Maggie told them she had put them on hold for a few months while she concentrated on something else, they just nodded acceptance and didn't pry.

The children treated her as they always had, expecting her to suggest games or help them with jigsaws, or read stories; and their parents hadn't changed so much that they no longer relied on her to keep them occupied on family occasions, but now it didn't bother Maggie. After all she liked the children and they liked her. She was even trying to write books for them for goodness sake; so playing with her own nephews and nieces was hardly a problem.

Determined to make a new start in every area of her life, she threw herself into the family Christmas with an enthusiasm that had been lacking for months, while at the same time making sure her mother didn't do too much and get over-tired.

When she sometimes felt a pang of loneliness as everyone else around her paired off, or when a casual mention of Ruairi or his mother prodded the wound in her heart, she pushed it to the back of her mind, focusing instead on her plans for the following year. Only June noticed the occasional glitter of tears and she was the only person who saw the deep down sadness in Maggie's soft grey eyes.

Chapter Seventeen

Ruairi's Christmas was far less successful. Racked with guilt about his mother as well as about the way he had treated Maggie, he wouldn't let himself celebrate. Instead he threw himself into his work, refusing all invitations to join the rest of the team on a trip to the nearest town for a pre-Christmas party.

On Christmas Day itself, there was a barbecue. The few colleagues, who, like Ruairi, lived too far away to get home for the festive season, organized it and given the hot sun and the idyllic setting, he should have enjoyed every minute of it. He didn't though because although he ate the food and tried to join in with the banter, his heart wasn't in it. For the first time in his career he wanted to be somewhere else. At that very moment he would willingly have swapped the sea, sun and sand for a bitter wind and icy rain if it meant he could be with Maggie, and he sat, nursing a glass of beer and thinking about it while the Christmas celebrations went on around him.

By the time the sun sank into the glittering sea he knew he had made a dreadful mistake, and by the time the Southern sky was filled with stars he was castigating himself for all kinds of a fool.

Why hadn't he gone with his heart? Why hadn't he trusted Maggie to make the right choice for her, for both of them? He remembered how she had felt in his arms, how she had kissed him freely and how her kiss had been full of love. Then he remembered her hurt expression when he told her she needed to live her own life and forget about him, and he wondered how he could have been so cruel. Somehow he had to get back to England to see her and tell her exactly how he felt, and when he did he just hoped she'd be able to forgive him for being so stupid.

Then he remembered how much work he still had to do to finish his documentary about the seals on time. He had to make preparations for his own penguin documentary too, so it would be close to Easter before he could travel back home. The three months of constant work stretching before him seemed like forever. Anything could happen to a girl like Maggie in three months. She was too bright and funny and beautiful to stay unattached for long. Maybe she had already found someone else and moved on.

At the thought his heart plummctcd, and when one of his colleagues asked him why he was looking so miserable he almost bit his head off. After that everyone left him alone to spend the rest of the night staring up at the sky and wishing he hadn't been such an idiot.

In a small, tight-knit team, news travels fast, however, so it wasn't long before a chance email to Ollie from one of the team mentioned that Ruairi was being uncharacteristically bad tempered and might even be depressed. He showed it to Jo.

"About time!" she said cryptically. Then she telephoned June.

Chapter Eighteen

When Mrs. O'Connor telephoned, Maggie was not altogether surprised. It was a call she was both looking forward to and dreading. It went better than she had anticipated, however, because the older woman was far too full of her own news to make any mention of Ruairi, and by the end of the call Maggie had agreed to go with her to view the bungalow she was hoping to buy.

"Would you like me to meet you at the airport?" she asked her towards the end of their conversation.

"Goodness me no, my dear. You'll be at work when the plane lands. I've got it all arranged. A car will meet me and I've booked three nights in a hotel. I've decided it's about time I learned to stand on my own feet."

Delighted that Mrs. O'Connor had got her old spark back, Maggie soon found she was looking forward to meeting her again, and she set out to pick her up from her hotel in high spirits.

* * *

The bungalow turned out to be just what she was looking for. It was light and airy with a small, enclosed garden that had obviously been much loved by its owners, and it was set in a quiet road right in the middle of four similar homes.

"I might even get a little dog to keep me company," Mrs. O'Connor said thoughtfully as they strolled around the neighboring roads after the viewing. "There's a park nearby, and a small piece of woodland just over the brow of that hill, so there would be plenty of places to walk a dog."

"Whatever has happened to the woman who refused to travel to England unless Ruairi brought her?" Maggie teased. "Now you're travelling on your own, and making plans to buy a dog too!"

"I am aren't I?" Mrs. O'Connor looked very pleased with herself. "I think it was learning how to work the computer that did it. Once Ruairi had proved to me that it wasn't difficult and persuaded me I would soon get the hang of it...well things just got better and better."

"Learning something new just gave you your confidence back," Maggie said. "And lots of people wouldn't have tried to learn in the first place, other people of..."

"My age! I know." Mrs. O'Connor burst out laughing when she saw how Maggie was mortified by her faux pas. "You're quite right my dear, I am old. I'd never have thought of learning to use a computer myself if Ruairi hadn't pushed me into it. Now…well I love it, and all I can say is that I feel sorry for those poor souls who don't have someone like him to look out for them."

I'm a poor soul too Maggie wanted to tell her, because I don't have Ruairi either. She didn't though. Instead she directed the conversation towards Mrs. O'Connor's moving plans, asking her how she was going to organize it.

The older woman shrugged it off. "I've plenty of time to think about that later because I can't move until the middle of the summer. The present owners are both teachers and they want to stay in the bungalow until the end of the school year when they'll have more time to organize the move. Besides, I still have to sell my home in Ireland. In the meantime though I've decided to take a little holiday with one of my oldest friends. We thought we'd go to Italy and visit Rome and Florence. They are places I've always wanted to see but because Tom didn't like city holidays, we never went."

"Goodness, you have changed," Maggie's eyes were wide with admiration. "Rome and Florence! How exciting!"

"Yes, it is. But first I want to invite you to stay with me in Ireland for a few days if you can spare the time, maybe at Easter. I know you like the countryside…well you did when you were a little girl… and although I'm determined to move back here I know I'll miss it. There's nowhere as beautiful as Southern Ireland and I'd love you to see it before I leave."

"But that's so kind of you," Maggie cried, touched by the invitation. "I'd love to visit you."

Mrs. O'Connor beamed at her in delight. "In that case I just need your Easter vacation dates. Once I have those I can organize my trip to Italy around them. I haven't booked it yet because I didn't want to be away at the very time you were free to visit."

* * *

The first half of the spring term seemed long and dreary, mainly due to a long spells of wet weather that kept the children indoors at break time when all they wanted to do was to play outside. A particularly virulent stomach bug also decimated the classrooms for days at a time, leaving the children tired and fractious when they returned to school.

Maggie, who had managed to avoid catching it, was very glad when the first signs of spring began to show themselves. She picked primroses from the garden and put them in a little pot on her desk to cheer everyone up.

She was still working hard, both at school and at home. The first draft of her book and some of the illustrations were now with the publisher and she was working hard on a second story. She was also trying, without much success, not to rush to the front door every time the postman pushed letters through the letterbox.

She had finally told Jo about her writing and been rewarded by the older girl's enthusiasm. Within moments she had called to Ollie to fetch a bottle of wine and some glasses from the kitchen, and soon they were drinking a toast to her success.

"But I might not be successful," she protested as she sipped her wine. "The publisher might send it back with a rejection slip."

"Doesn't matter," Jo told her. "It's the fact you are doing it that counts. Writing and drawing as often as you can fit it in is what will make you successful whether it's now or in a few years time. Besides, the publishers wouldn't have asked to see your work if they weren't impressed with the ideas in your enquiry letter."

"What sort of illustrations do you do?" asked Ollie. He'd shaved off his beard now he was living an urban life but it didn't make a lot of difference. He still looked as if he was only marking time until he could return to the great outdoors, and turning to answer his question, Maggie's heart lurched as she suddenly realized it wouldn't be many more months before her new friends were on the other side of the globe again. With Ruairi.

Pushing the thought to the back of her mind, to the small dark space labeled Ruairi that she tried not to open, she concentrated on answering him.

"Animals and birds mostly," she said. "Anything to do with nature really, although I sometimes add small children and buildings and a few other things. It all depends on the story."

"And if you are successful will you give up teaching?"

"I don't know...I haven't really thought about it. A decision as big as that would have to depend on how successful I become. The publisher is very enthusiastic about the stuff I've sent, but I still might turn out to be a one-book wonder. Besides, I enjoy teaching."

Jo gave her a severe look. "That's enough negativity for one day. Just think of the benefits if you are successful. For one thing you'll be able to visit us any time you like because a writer can work anywhere can't they?"

"I guess so, but you really are jumping the gun Jo. I can't start thinking of things like that yet. Thinking positive is one thing, talking about throwing away my career is another."

"Who's talking about throwing it away? You could just do it differently...become somebody who organizes writing workshops or visits schools to talk to the children about writing stories. Maybe you could even demonstrate how you illustrate your books. That way you'd have the best of both worlds."

"Is she always like this?" Maggie asked Ollie.

He grinned at her. "Always! If Jo has decided you are going to be a successful children's author then that's what you're going to be. She has got a point though. Think of the freedom it would give you. You could go anywhere. Travel to other countries and write stories about their wildlife too, that sort of thing."

"I love it that you both have so much faith in me but don't expect me to rush off into the wild blue yonder straight away will you. There will plenty of time for that in the future if your totally baseless convictions come true."

She bent over to tickle Henry's feet as she spoke, so she didn't see the fleeting glance that passed between Jo and Ollie. And when he eventually excused himself, saying he had to get on with his work, she couldn't know that the first thing Ollie did was to fire an email off to Ruairi.

Chapter Nineteen

Easter finally arrived in a burst of sunshine. Everyone immediately cheered up, and by the time her father dropped her off at the airport for her flight to Ireland, Maggie was full of excited anticipation. She had also just learned that her first book was going to be published later in the year, and she couldn't wait to tell Mrs. O'Connor about it.

At Jo's suggestion she packed pencils, watercolors and a notebook into the beautiful flight bag she'd finally felt strong enough to retrieve from the back of her wardrobe. It had the strange effect of making her feel as if she were going on a working holiday rather than to visit an elderly woman who had been kind to her when she was a little girl. She gave a wry smile as she zipped it shut. What a difference a little bit of positive thinking made. In a few short months she'd acquired a publisher and had new career mapped out, even though she couldn't afford to give up teaching yet. The whole family was proud of her too, especially her mother. She kept telling everyone who would listen how she'd always known her beautiful daughter had talent. Only one thing was missing from Maggie's life. Ruairi. She sighed as she picked up the burgundy-colored flight bag and hurried out to where her father was waiting for her in his car. No amount of positive thinking was going to change that, so she may as well get used to it.

Although the flight was a bit bumpy due to low cloud, it didn't delay the plane, and in what only seemed to be minutes, it was skimming over the treetops to touch down in Ireland. True to her promise, Mrs. O'Connor was waiting for her. She introduced her to the tall, rangy man standing at her side.

"This is my neighbor Patrick Duggan. Patrick, this is Maggie."

Patrick Duggan smiled at her, his eyes full of appreciation. "You didn't tell me that it was a beauty I'd be meeting, Moira. With that face I'm guessing she's related to you."

"Well you're guessing wrong you old flatterer," she told him, laughing at Maggie's pink cheeks. "She's a dear girl who I've known for most of her life but we're not related. Her beauty is all her own."

He chuckled as he picked up Maggie's suitcase as if weighed no more than a feather and led the way outside.

"Patrick was coming into town today anyway," Mrs. O'Connor explained as they followed him. "He and his wife have been very good to me since Tom died. The only trouble is that they are so busy all day running their farm that I hardly see them. It's one of the reasons I'm coming back to England. I need to be with people who have time for coffee in the mornings and a good gossip."

Maggie laughed. "Then please take my mother in hand. She needs someone like you to slow her down. Coffee mornings would be ideal. She spends far too much time worrying about the family."

"I know. It comes with being a mother," Mrs. O'Connor shook her head as they made their way across the car park. "I've had to learn to stop worrying about Ruairi. I've had to accept that he's quite capable of leading his own life but it's been difficult. Really difficult."

Maggie refused to be drawn on Ruairi. She had already steeled herself in preparation for the photographs she was sure would be all around the house. She knew there would be discussions about him too, but she wasn't going to initiate them. Swiftly she changed the subject, asking about the journey to the cottage, whether it was very far, and what they would see on the way.

Mrs. O'Connor didn't appear to mind and before long she was pointing out landmarks and giving Maggie a potted history of the area as Patrick drove them home.

* * *

The cottage was lovely. Painted white, it was set on a hillside above a small bay with a wonderful view of the sea and the hills. Instantly Maggie knew it was a place where she could work, and as she had the thought she

229

remembered Jo's words about how she could do things differently if she tried. Looking at everything around her she wondered if her friend was right. The scenery was an inspiration in itself because there were ancient hedgerows to paint, and clusters of wild flowers, and quirky cottages, and sweet faced cows standing in the fields. And they were all things she would never see if she stayed at home, teaching class-after-class of five-year-olds as the years rolled by. Maybe it was time to make some real plans for the future, ones that included new horizons, because she couldn't remember when she had last felt so excited about something, and her fingers itched to get started.

Restraining herself with difficulty, she admired the cottage and the cozy bedroom Mrs. O'Connor had made ready for her. It's window was set high up in the roof, giving her one of the best views of the bay, and she felt she could sit there for hours gazing at the scenery while her mind grappled with the theme for another book.

* * *

Over the next few days Maggie and Mrs. O'Connor settled into a routine that suited thcm both. As soon as she had finished a breakfast of fruit, soda bread spread thick with Irish butter and honey, and two cups of tea, Maggie would set off with her sketchbook and drawing materials. While she was away Mrs. O'Connor listened to the radio as she tidied the house and prepared lunch.

In the afternoons Maggie would show her what she had drawn in her notebook and then, while the older woman sewed, she would get out her paints and add the colors of the countryside to her sketches.

Later, when they had put away their work, they would sit in the tiny conservatory that had been added to the side of the house and drink a glass of wine while they watched the sun slide into the sea.

From the moment Maggie arrived Mrs. O'Connor had made it very clear to her that she was in Ireland for a holiday and she had shooed her out of the kitchen whenever she tried to help. Recognizing that her friend was enjoying having someone to care for after being on her own for so long, Maggie gave in gratefully and spent the time when she wasn't sketching and painting, reading, or just sitting and looking at the view and letting the peace of the place wash over her.

Too fired up by the need to paint the beauty all around her to keep it to herself for a moment longer, she had told Mrs. O'Connor, on the very first evening, about the book that had just been accepted by a publisher, and of her dream of a full time career writing and illustrating children's books. The older woman's response had been so intensely gratifying that Maggie wished she had told her about her ambitions months before.

"In that case you must spend as much time as you want drawing and painting," she had told her. "I'm just pleased to have company around the house; someone to bake for. And I'll enjoy seeing your drawings too."

And she had. She had even made some very practical suggestions and told Maggie where to find hidden glens and shallow streams, and clusters of newly unfurled bright green ferns; the sort of places that were exactly right for Maggie's picture book. And once she had sketched and painted them, Moira O'Connor's admiration and enthusiasm was such music to her ears that she wondered why she had kept her dreams a secret from everyone for so long.

Because you were frightened people would laugh at you the little dark voice that still occasionally invaded her thoughts told her. *You thought they would just say it was another of your whims, not to be taken seriously.*

The thought spurred her into greater action because she knew now that she was good, that her drawings, so carefully stored away for so long, were the fledgling steps of talented illustrator, and she was determined to do herself justice.

* * *

Strangely, although she had dreaded seeing photos of Ruairi everywhere and having to listen to stories about his childhood, or about the work he was doing now, it wasn't as bad as she had expected. For one thing there were only a couple of framed photos and they were both several years old, so it was almost as if the Ruairi she was in love with didn't exist. And although his mother did refer to him occasionally, it was in such a casual way that Maggie wasn't obliged to continue the conversation.

So when she went down to the kitchen on the sixth morning of her stay she was feeling more relaxed than she would have thought possible just a few months earlier. Smiling her thanks as her hostess poured her a mug of tea, she sat at the table and admired the stripes of early morning sunlight dappling the quarry tiles on the floor.

Mrs. O'Connor pushed the breadboard towards her so she could cut off a chunk of freshly baked soda bread. "I've been thinking," she said. "It's set to be another lovely day so why don't I pack you up a picnic. Then you'll be able to wander a bit further afield when you're sketching today."

"But that doesn't seem fair. Not when I've come to visit you," Maggie protested.

"Nonsense my dear! I just like to see you enjoying yourself. And it's not often we have such a long spell of uninterrupted sunshine. The weatherman on the radio forecast high temperatures for the rest of the week, so make the most of it while you have the chance. Besides, I have one or two things to do today, and I'm expecting a visitor too."

"Well if you're really sure then I would love to spend the day walking," Maggie told her, and before long she was packing food and a flask into a small rucksack alongside her sketchpad.

She set off full of excited anticipation. Mrs. O'Connor watched from the open doorway of the cottage until she was out of sight and then she swiftly cleared the breakfast things from the table, tidied the kitchen and, with an anxious glance at the clock, hurried upstairs.

Chapter Twenty

A practiced traveler, Ruairi was the first one off the plane when it touched down, and he was waiting at the luggage carousel long before the suitcases came tumbling through. Within moments he had piled his own luggage onto a trolley and pushed it through to the arrivals concourse to where a hire car was waiting.

He barely saw the wonderful scenery as he drove along the coast to his mother's cottage. Instead he kept rehearsing all the things he wanted to say to Maggie; things he'd been writing and re-writing in his head ever since this hair-brained idea had been conceived.

It was all very well for June and Jo, using Ollie as their go-between, to tell him he just needed to spend time with Maggie away from her family if he was serious about her. It was all very well for them to persuade his mother to invite Maggie to stay with her and not tell him about it until his travel dates were confirmed. They weren't going to be at the receiving end. What if Maggie didn't want to see him? What if she couldn't forgive him? What if she decided to take the next plane back to England before he had a chance to tell her how he felt about her?

He was still full of the dark thoughts that had filled his mind ever since he had finally realized he'd been a fool to leave Maggie behind, when he finally pulled up outside his mother's cottage and killed the engine.

She was waiting for him in the doorway with an anxious frown that turned into a huge smile of welcome as soon as she saw him. He reached her in two strides and swept her into a bear hug that almost lifted her from the ground.

She smiled up at him. "I think you'd better smarten yourself up or Maggie won't recognize you."

He rubbed his hands over the stubble on his face with a groan. "I feel as if I've been travelling for days…and I'd kill for a cup of coffee."

"Go and have a shower and freshen up while I cook you bacon and eggs. You need something decent to eat after twenty four hours of airline food."

* * *

Thirty minutes later, showered and shaved, he was sitting down to a piled plateful of food that he washed down with several cups of strong coffee. Not until he had finished did he ask the question that had been uppermost in his mind from the moment he left New Zealand.

"How's Maggie?" He gave his mother a wry smile, embarrassed by his reluctance to talk about the very thing he held most dear.

236

"Maggie's fine," she told him calmly.

"Does she know I'm here?"

"She does not."

He stared at her. "You're not going to tell me a thing are you?"

"No!"

Then she softened slightly. "Whatever did or didn't happen between you and Maggie is your business Ruairi. I have no rights on how you live your life, nor do I expect to have, so I am only going to give you one piece of advice."

He waited.

"Don't break that poor girl's heart again. And once she's forgiven you, don't take no for an answer or you'll regret it for the rest of your life!"

He grinned at her. "You said one thing, that's two!"

"So it is. Well you'd better go and look for her before I think of something else. She was going to walk over the headland but she'll probably be on her way back by now. She's wearing a red jacket and she's carrying a small rucksack, so you'll know it's her, even at a distance."

He pushed back his chair, stood up, dropped a kiss on the top of her head and walked out of the cottage without another word.

She shook her head as she watched him go. He might have travelled the world and found himself fame and fortune in his chosen career, but when it came to his heart he still had a lot to learn.

* * *

As Ruairi strode across the fields he felt his heart lift. His mother had said when Maggie forgives you, so she must think he had a chance. Not that he would have chosen to do it this way. He'd had a much more subtle plan in mind, one that involved a telephone conversation, an invitation to dinner, a gentle approach that he hoped would undo the hurt he had caused. But thanks to his friends and his mother it was an option that had been taken away. Unless he was going to leave the country again he had to face Maggie the hard way. No props, no romantic lighting or soft music, just him and Maggie with the memories of the past between them. He'd felt sick with anxiety for days, so sure had he been she would reject him; but now, with a soft breeze blowing up from the sea, and the sun highlighting the distant mountains, he suddenly felt more optimistic. Maybe it would work after all.

* * *

He had been walking for almost thirty minutes before he saw her and even then it was only a flash of red out of the corner of his eye. Turning his head swiftly he was just in time to catch a distant glimpse of her outlined against the sky before she plunged down a hillside and out of sight.

Changing direction he began to jog, anxious to cut across her path before he lost her. She was further away than he realized though, so by the time he saw her again she was on the beach. He paused at the top of the path leading down to the bay, his heart thudding against his chest, not from exertion but from the sudden sight of Maggie sitting with her back against a rock, a sketchpad resting on her knee. As he watched he saw her hand move swiftly across the paper, shaping and shading as she reproduced the view in front of her.

How long he stood there he never knew. It could have been hours or minutes because, for Ruairi, time stood still as he gazed down at the woman he loved and wondered all over again how he could ever have been stupid enough to walk away from her.

Finally she finished drawing and slipping her sketchpad into her rucksack, she stood up. Ruairi took a deep breath and readied himself for the rejection he was afraid he might see in her face but instead of picking up her belongings, Maggie wandered off towards the edge of the bay, away from him. She seemed to be searching for shells because every now and again she would pick one up and study it. Mostly she threw them away again but occasionally she would keep one, slipping it into the pocket of her jacket before moving on.

Ruairi watched the graceful movements of her body as she bent and sifted through a pile of stones, or used her foot, clad in a sturdy walking boot, to push at something the tide had left at the water's edge. He noticed the way the wind tugged at her hair so that wisps escaped from the clips she had used to restrain it and blew across her face. He saw how agile she was as she clambered across some scattered rocks to peer into a rock pool. And then, finally, she turned, and he saw her face.

It was everything he remembered, and more. Despite the distance between them he could see the high curve of her cheekbones and the smoothness of her brow, and as she came nearer he saw how the sun had warmed her cheeks to a flushed pink and burnished the skin at her throat to a pale gold. Then, as the sea breeze tugged at her unfastened jacket and uncovered the curves he had tried to erase from his mind, he almost stopped breathing.

When he finally regained his senses, he opened his mouth to call to her. At the exact same moment she looked up and saw him and for a long, long moment they stared at one another across the width of the small bay. Then she smiled, and with a great leap of his heart he knew it was going to be all right.

* * *

By the time they returned to the cottage the light was fading and a chill wind was beginning to blow in from the sea. Neither of them noticed it though. They were too wrapped up in one another as they trudged across the fields, mostly

240

talking, although occasionally Ruairi brought them to a stop so he could kiss her again.

"I can't believe I was so stupid," he told her as he brushed wayward strands of copper colored hair from her face.

"Ssh! It's over now," Maggie put her fingers across his lips and then stood on tiptoe so that she could kiss the corner of his mouth.

He groaned, pulling her towards him with a sudden impatience that she quickly matched, her fingers creeping up into the hair that curled at the nape of his neck. It was a long time before they moved on after that but when they did Ruairi picked up the conversation he had interrupted.

"I didn't think I was ready to settle down. There's still so much I want to do and, stupidly, I thought getting married would interfere with that."

Maggie dragged him to an abrupt halt. "Married! I don't recall a marriage proposal or did I miss something?"

He stared down at her in surprise. "Of course we're getting married. That was half my problem in the first place. I knew I couldn't have a casual relationship with you. It knew it had to be all or nothing, and like a fool I almost chose nothing."

Maggie gazed up at him speechlessly. Would she ever understand him? Why had it taken him seven months on the other side of the world to see sense when she had known what she wanted from almost the moment she first saw him? Then she remembered what she had been like seven months earlier and knew she had been partly responsible for sending him away. She had spent too much time telling him how dissatisfied she was with her life. She had been over sensitive and prickly in turns, with no real plans for her future, just a muddle of dreams and wishes. The Maggie of seven months earlier had been far too self obsessed and immature to cope with the lifestyle Ruairi was offering her.

"I wasn't ready," she told him, staring down at the buttons on his jacket so she didn't have to look at him as she tried to find the right words. "I didn't have any real plans. I thought I did but I didn't, not really. And I didn't know enough about people either. Seven months ago I would have been a liability."

"And now?"

She heard the laughter in his voice and then his finger was under her chin, lifting her face up to his. As he lowered his lips, he said it again.

"Oh now! Now I'm definitely an asset," she said and then she didn't say anything else for a very long time.

When they finally broke away Maggie's mouth was plump and moist with desire. Ruairi's clear hazel eyes darkened to the color of peat as he gazed down at her. Then he smiled.

"I'll take that as a yes then," he said.

* * *

It was almost dark when they reached the cottage and Maggie was the first one to notice there were no lights on. Anxiously she turned to Ruairi.

"Your mother would normally have switched on the kitchen light by now, and pulled the curtains in the sitting room. Do you think she's all right?"

"She's probably having a nap or watching the television or something," he told her, but nevertheless he lengthened his stride until Maggie had to run to keep up with him.

When they pushed open the kitchen door all was silent. Worried more than she cared to say, Maggie switched on the light.

"Where do you think she is?" she asked Ruairi, her voice shaking slightly.

But he was already unfolding a note that was propped against the kettle. Maggie watched his face as he scanned it, sure something was dreadfully wrong, and so she was startled when he started to laugh in big, hearty guffaws that rang across the cozy kitchen. Then he thrust the note at her.

Maggie stared at it in disbelief. It was short and very much to the point.

Gone to Italy. Back in 10 days.
Love to you both xx
P.S. Casserole in oven just needs reheating.

When Ruairi had finally stopped chuckling he gathered Maggie into his arms. "Things have certainly changed around here while I've been away. My Mother now surfs the internet and organizes foreign holidays without any help from me, and I have a fiancée who is a children's author and illustrator. What happened?"

"We both grew up and learned to be brave," Maggie told him with a smile. Then she gave a cry of indignation.

"Whatever is the matter now?" Ruairi pulled her hands away from her face, concern deep in his eyes.

"Now I'm not going travelling on my own anymore, no-one in my family will ever believe I've grown up enough to run my own life. They will always see me as tag-along Maggie, with you looking after me the same as you did when I was small."

"No they won't," he said. "Besides I can think of a lot of things you can do to prove you are very grown up indeed."

And when Maggie looked up at him, her eyes full of questions, he bent down and whispered in her ear. Then he laughed at the blush that suffused her face, swung her up into his arms, and headed towards the stairs.

Epilogue

"Come on. There are far more important things to do than unpack," Ruairi pulled Maggie away from her suitcase and propelled her towards the open door.

She started to protest. Then she saw the expression in his eyes and decided against it. Whatever Ruairi wanted to do, it was obviously very important to him. She put her hand into his and followed him outside.

He led her away from the square cabin with the tin roof that was to be their home for the next six months, and on down a sandy path to the sea. When they stepped onto the beach she gazed about her with delight. The bright moon revealed a wide stretch of silver sand with a backdrop of tufted dunes. Dunes that she knew hid the burrows of the tiny blue penguins Ruairi was filming for his documentary: the penguins who were also going to feature in her next book.

She was filled with a huge sense of excitement as she thought about the three-book contract she'd signed with her publisher a few days before travelling to New Zealand.

"I can hardly bear to wait until tomorrow," she told him. "There is so much I want to see, and do. So many things I want to draw."

He smiled down at her. "There's plenty of time for all of that. Don't rush into tomorrow when there is still the best of today."

Then he pulled her down beside him and made her lie back on the sand. She stared up at him, her eyes and hair striped silver by the moonlight, her lips slightly parted. She was used to Ruairi now and she welcomed his sudden passions, his lack of convention. She was so secure in his love that she knew she would be able to cope when he had to go away, and she was so full of love for him that she was prepared to follow him to the ends of the earth if necessary.

He kissed her slowly and thoroughly and then, to her surprise, he rolled away from her. "Now look up," he said.

She tilted her head so she could gaze up at the southern sky, and when she saw the huge nebula of the Milky Way surrounded by the glitter of millions and trillions of stars, unexpected tears trickled down her cheeks.

"It's so beautiful Ruairi. It looks like it might have looked when earth was dawning," she told him.

Hearing her echo his own unspoken thoughts he felt an immense sense of gratitude. Marrying Maggie had made him whole. She was his other half; the part of him he hadn't realized was missing until it was almost too late. He leaned across and kissed away her tears. And after that they lay there for a long, long time, fingers and hearts entwined.

The End

If you enjoyed this book, please leave a review.

Other Books We Love books by Sheila Claydon

Cabin Fever
Reluctant Date
Double Fault
Kissing Maggie Silver
Mending Jodie's Heart (When Paths Meet Book 1)
Finding Bella Blue (When Paths Meet Book 2)
Saving Katy Gray (When Paths Meet Book 3)
Miss Locatelli
Remembering Rose (Mapleby Memories Book 1)
The Sheila Claydon Special Edition
The Hollywood Collection

In the 1980s Sheila Claydon wrote a number of romances under the pseudonym Anne Beverley. Then a busy career and family life got in the way and before she knew it, she had turned her back on the characters who were begging to be liberated from her imagination. Now she is back to writing fiction again and, considerably older and no longer shy, writes under her own name.

Her motto is a quote by the late Ray Bradbury: "First, find out what your hero wants. Then just follow him."

Although family remains central to her life, she still finds the time to read, to write, and to travel. Many of the places she has visited feature in her books. Her fans say that reading them is like buying a ticket to romance.

You can find her at

https://www.facebook.com/SheilaClaydon.author/

www.ingramcontent.com/pod-product-compliance
Lightning Source LLC
Chambersburg PA
CBHW051637260626
47170CB00004B/1213